Time, Trial, Trust

Geneva Kpangbai Diwan

ISBN: 1542853737
ISBN-13: 9781542853736

DEDICATION

This book is dedicated to my family and friends and you. Pursing your dreams takes courage, discipline and hard work but regardless of how much time, effort, and sacrifice it may take; you owe it to yourself to pursue your dreams. Only you can make your dreams a reality. Please do!

CONTENTS

ACKNOWLEDGMENTS

I want to acknowledge those who helped me on my literary journey in one way or another. There is no specific order of importance; I am simply writing as the names comes to my mind. I do not want to forget anyone but it's possible that I might, so please forgive me if I do not mention you by name. I am beyond excited to be done with writing the story and I'm just glad to finally be able to write this part. Michel'le Brown, girl you were the very first person I shared "Time, Trial, Trust" with. I remember it was some time in 2014, June perhaps and we went on our lunch break and ate in my car. I pulled out my phone and read you the preface; the first and only thing I had written. You said "What's that?" I said "It's my book I'm going to write. Do you like it?" You said "Yeah I'll read it". Thank you for listening. You've been supportive ever since. To Lela Simpson thank you for lending me your laptop for weeks on end when I didn't own one so I could start typing up the story. There were times you had to do your assignments and you'd come to my house to pick up the laptop but you always brought it back so I could continue writing. It was like we both owned *your* laptop until I could finally afford to buy one of my own. Xavier, when I finally had the money to purchase a laptop you came through and hooked up Microsoft word on it for a very *very* small fee. I am truly computer illiterate when it comes to things like that and I sure did not know how to do it. Thank you for installing it. It allowed me to continue writing from the comfort of my own home. To Sasha Medina; Sasha you need your own page for this acknowledgement. First let me start by saying thank you for recommending and or convincing your brother Xavier to install Microsoft word for me. I truly believe if God had not sent you in my life I would still be struggling on how to complete this book. Other than actually writing the story you did everything else! I mean everything! You were my editor, motivator, confidant, friend, and so much more! Thank you for being readily available whenever I needed to vent about the frustrations of life and writing. You never judged, you always listened. Your advice, ideas, recommendations, and suggestions were all extremely helpful. From the moment I told you I was writing a book, you made it your personal mission to help me every step of the way and that is exactly what you did! You made it possible for this book to be tangible. I honestly cannot thank you enough. You did so many things and if I try to list them all I won't have room to acknowledge other people. To Mama Nicole aka Nicole Bush, I know you believe in me because you said when you own your bookstore (and you will), my book would be in it. When I told you I was writing a book you said "Good. I love to see young people accomplishing their dreams." I accomplished it Mama Nicole. Thank you for believing in me; not only are you my best friend

Mama, you have become a mama to me also. To Ryan Scott-Bush aka Ry aka Hunnii aka my best friend! From the moment we met and begin having endless girl talk and I told you I wanted to write a book you said "Do it Gee! You can do it! Ain't nothing to it but just to do it!" Thank you for your support Ry and for saying, "Email it to me Gee so I can read it." Oh yes girl thanks for those chit chats, it came in handy when I needed a break from writing or a motivation to keep writing. To Emily Awopeju; Em I knew you wanted to just go home after church but I would ask you to stay a little longer when you visited me on Sundays so I could read a chapter or so from the book. You were tired but you always stayed whenever I asked you to; thank you for staying and listening. Also thank you for encouraging me when I text you saying, "I'm so over this writing thing. I just want to be done already." Your exact words were "You got this" thanks Em I appreciate you. To Pastor Clara, you are more than the person who help me with spiritual guidance, you are also my confidant and you believe in me so much! Thank you for all you've done for me. I love the way you celebrated over the phone with me when I called and told you I completed the book. You were genuinely happy for me. To the men who broke my heart aka my ex's thank you for the experiences; I learned from them. To my amazing, loving, and caring husband Isaac Diwan, baby thank you for your patience with me through everything. Thank you for doing the household chores while I focused on writing. You are simply the best. Your love for me shows and I am reminded everyday by all the things you do for me just how much you love me. I love you too! Thanks for encouraging and supporting me babe. Those pillow talks truly worked! To my Mama thank you for birthing me! Even though we are millions of miles away from each other, thank you for always being in touch with me, I love you mama! To my colleagues at

Children's Friend, Carter Street building Head Start, you ladies all rock! Every single one of you! Thanks for your support. To my cousins Marie and Nikki I love you both. Marie when I read you a section from the book you said, "Cous that sounds really good." You had me feeling like real deal writer. I guess I am huh? Nikki you keep me laughing and you certainly do encourage me whenever we talk; thanks Cousin Nikki. To the people who I mentioned to that I was writing a book and would ask on occasion "How's the book going?" Thanks for doing that. Your concern reminded me to keep writing. My husband once told me a saying "If you want to get somewhere fast go alone if you want to get far, go with somebody" or something like that, he tells me a lot of sayings. The bottom line is I could not have gone as far as I did with this book; so far as to actually completing it if it was not for each and everyone that I listed. Again I am terribly sorry if I did not list you by name. Please know that I appreciate your contribution to my writing journey. Forgive me.

Thank you Lord God Almighty for blessing me with

many gifts and talents but especially the gift of writing!

With you all things are possible and you alone have

made this book possible. Thank you Jesus!

Credits

Photographer: Leonard K. Dougbe

Instagram(Indsstudios)

Facebook (INDSSTUDIOS)

Cover girl: Emily Awopeju

Preface

Smelling the sweet aroma of hazelnut coffee foaming through the cracks of her bedroom door, Delanie got out of bed and slipped on her silky white robe with pink fluffy house slippers. It was 5:30am and she was surprised that Tyson was up this early on a Saturday morning *and* making coffee at that. Reluctantly dragging her feet, she strolled into the kitchen where her eyes met this six foot, chocolate, well-cut biceps, giant standing shirtless in the middle of their kitchen. His pearl white smile cut sleep residues right out of her eyes as he gently embraced her, placing long wet kisses on her lips.

"Good morning, Sunshine. I made your coffee." he said.

Smiling but still a little puzzled she took a sip of the rich, creamy, better than Starbucks coffee.

"Hmmm...good morning indeed." she said shocked.

"Baby, what are you doing up at this time?" she asked.

As a mechanical engineer Tyson worked Monday

through Friday and had the weekends off. Still smiling in between taking sips of her coffee she stared at him amazed by how surprisingly sweet he could be at times. This was a nice surprise especially knowing how much he loved to sleep in on Saturdays.

Delanie thought about how time flies; a year ago she and Tyson exchanged vows at a very small intimate ceremony at their local church. 365 days later she was still on cloud nine.

"Well, I know how much you don't totally look forward to working on Saturdays." Tyson Said.

"Hmm…continue."

"So I thought it would be kind of me to make you a cup of coffee to help cheer you up. Plus I have something else I would like to give you and I thought this would be a good way to wake you up," he replied.

Delanie gave him the "I know what this is about look" but before she could utter the words he picked her up and escorted her back to their bedroom with the scent of coffee trailing behind them.

"So this was your plan? Caffeine me up and take advantage of me?" she said jokingly. They both laughed as she braced her mind for the heavenly encounter that was about to take place between them.

Chapter
- One -

Light Rain

Grayish milky clouds roamed above as trinkets of
water fell slowly from the sky sliding off her
windshields. Delanie sat in her car listening to the
sound of rain instead of the intensive beating of her
heart. She stepped out and let her bare brown feet hit
the cold wet pavement of the parking lot and sank her
toes into small puddles. She had lost track of time.
How long has she been sitting in the car? Did her tears
stop flowing? Delanie did not know. None of it
mattered. Delanie longed for the touches of rain as she
leaned her back against the driver's door feeling the
cold slippery glass on her upper back. She stood and
watched the tiny water bubbles form and dissipate off
her non-melting chocolate skin. Delanie wished the
rain could pour down heavier. She needed to feel
something other than the left over punches resulting
from yet another altercation with Ernest. The washing
away of her pain would take more than a few drizzles

18

of rain water.

Delanie wished she could stand in the parking lot for eternity. The clouds were growing darker and she was beginning to feel cold. She locked her car door and walked back into her dorm room. Her cell phone rang the minute she stepped foot into the room. Without allowing her to say 'hello' Ernest spoke. "I'm so sorry girl. I'm just so stressed. I don't know what came over me. You just make me so mad! I don't know why you won't just listen to me," Ernest's voice echoed through the semi-wet cell phone which Delanie held mid-way to her ears.

This had to be the fifteen-millionth time she had heard the same line of sorry easing from his mouth. His 'sorry's' no longer phased her. She was accustomed to picking out every other word that proceeded from Ernest's mouth. Delanie cringed whenever he said the word 'girl'. It bothered her, in her mind girl meant innocent, naïve, stupid, young, not capable of making profound decisions. Was that what she had become? Granted she was young but the last time she checked eighteen was the legal adult age. No she was not a girl! She was an adult. Delanie wondered why Ernest could not see her as such. Did he really think she was just a girl? A child? Someone who needed to be reprimanded? *His* child? Delanie no longer wanted to be a girl and certainly not his *girl.* They were supposed to be boyfriend and girlfriend, lovers, in love. She was not his punching bag.

"Please Delanie can I come over? I want to make it up to you," Ernest's raspy voice continued sending feelings of disgust through her.

Delanie looked around the one hundred and fourteen or so square foot dorm room. Suddenly it dawned on her why these room were so small and could only fit a twin size bed.

"I have to study for an exam. Let's just talk about it tomorrow please," she lied.

Before Ernest could say another word she hung up. If she listened for another second Ernest would say some magical words which would suck her back into his arms. Delanie needed to rest, cry, and maybe even think. She plopped her body on the oversized lime green bean bag chair which sat in the left corner of the room. Her wet black tube top dress was stuck to her skin. The inside of her arms displayed the imprints of Ernest's fingers. Sitting up on the bean bag, that little voice rang inside her head, *break it off.*

Fresh Start

"Yes. Okay. Thank you. See you in two weeks," Delanie hung up the phone and screamed. Running out of her bedroom, Kaydence rushed into the living room. "Did you get it?!" Jumping and hopping like an anxious five year old. "Yes girl! I start in two weeks!" In unison they both screamed "Yaayyyyy!" Delanie had just landed a job as a case worker for a company called "Fresh Start" the job had come at an opportune time in her life. Having graduated college with a Bachelors in Human Services it had been difficult for her to find a job she really wanted in her field. She had been working full time as a manager at a local supermarket but for the past two months now she had contemplated on quitting. Delanie thought she might have to hang on to the supermarket because a week ago she signed the lease to her new apartment. After a year of living with her best friend of thirteen years it was time for her to be in her own space. Taking a leap of faith she decided to update her resume and search for a job in her field. A day after she sent her resume in, she received a call from Fresh Start, went on the interview and had now been offered the position. It seemed fitting for Delanie to work for Fresh Start. The company was founded by a native West African woman. She established the company to assist families from West Africa as well as other minorities to smoothly transition into life in the United States.

Delanie researched the company and felt passionate about working there because she too was undergoing life's transitions.

"I'm so excited for you Dee. Everything is happening so fast. I wished we could live together forever," Kaydence said sitting on the couch next to Delanie. "Now you know that's a lie. You know I was working your last nerve, or at least you were working mine," Delanie softly pushed Kaydence. As much as the two women loved each other and enjoyed living together, having endless "girl talk" they both had to agree that it was time for Delanie to be in her own place. Delanie was beyond grateful to have a sister-friend like Kaydence who stepped in when everything in her life took a toll for the worse. Plenty of so called friends walked out on her, gossiping behind her back saying how much of a fool she was, but not Kaydence. It was like she knew eventually this moment was going to happen.

Although Delanie did not have much to pack other than her clothes, a few books, and some household essentials she bought for the apartment yet packing still proved to be a daunting task. She had scheduled for her furniture and bedroom set to be delivered on a Saturday one week after she moved in. She paid movers to deliver the things because other than Kaydence there was no one who could help her and there was certainly no way she and Kaydence could drive a moving truck, pick up furniture, haul it into the apartment and put everything together. They were strong women but not *that* strong. That type of work demanded for some man power which they clearly did not possess.

"Kaydence can you please grab my pink duffle bag from the back seat?" Delanie hollered out of the kitchen window to her best friend just as she was about to close the passenger door and bring the last suitcase into the apartment. "Girl, you are lucky I got love for you because you are truly working me like a slave," Kaydence grunted pulling the suitcase with the duffle bag tossed over her shoulder. She locked the car and made her way up to the second floor. Finally after what seemed like eternity the two ladies were done hauling all of the things upstairs into Delanie's new apartment. "I forgot how much work moving is, I need a glass of water or something," Kaydence walked over to the refrigerator and grabbed a bottle of Poland Spring, without stopping to breathe in between drinks, she guzzled down the entire bottle. Thankfully Delanie bought a case of water and placed some in the fridge when she first received the key. Staring at her own apartment with boxes and suitcases everywhere, Delanie skipped over a small box marked "bathroom" and swung her arms around Kaydence nearly knocking her over. As she tightly embraced her friend, streams of hot tears rolled down her face. "Oh Dee don't do that, this is it. You deserve this," Kaydence said feeling the droplets of tears down her bare shoulders. The two women both stood speechlessly in the middle of the kitchen with tears flowing out of their eyes. These were happy tears. Tears of relief that now life was about to begin again. Delanie was excited to begin this life with so much anticipation for what her future held. It certainly did not bother her that for the next seven days she'd spend her nights sleeping on the hard floor with only a comforter and pillow but the thought of her finally sleeping in her own place comforted her.

Change

The freedom of the highway always brought Delanie joy. She enjoyed driving non-stop with her windows down as intense breeze flowed in and out of her car. Living in the smallest state, everyone in Rhode Island only drove fifty miles per hour. But today Delanie was breaking the speed limit, driving as fast as those thousand thoughts that were running through her mind while making her way down interstate 95 North to see Dr. Summers in Milford, Massachusetts. Fortunately Massachusetts has a speed limit of sixty-five miles per hour on the freeway. Every so often her mind would drift to the events of her life which had cost her to take these frequent drives down to Massachusetts. As she drove, Delanie remembered the scenario like it was yesterday when she had an emotional break down at the Providence Place mall in one of their favorite stores. *It was senior year of their college career and the girls were doing their weekly shopping trips for an "All White" campus party. They browsed through the store trying on several pieces of clothing. The exciting part of college was the night life. The girls enjoyed pre-gaming in their dorms then getting all dolled-up and strolling their way through campus in their six-inches heals. Although majoring in Early Childhood Education, Kaydence was a fashion fanatic* and a make-up artist in the making. She loved all things fashion. Delanie on the other hand was a little bit more conservative with her style but that was before she began to reluctantly allow Kaydence to give her a few "fashion tips" whenever they were about to venture off on one of their night life scenes.

Kaydence was glad to have her friend back after the break-up with Ernest.

"Girllll! That dress is hot! Fire and desire!" Kaydence told her, examining the backless white sequin dress on Delanie.

Delanie stood with her hands on her waist as tears welled up in her eyes hitting the floor. Instantly almost panting she let out a loud cry. Kaydence held her confused and shocked as workers rushed to the door knocking and asking if everything was okay. This was not the first time Delanie had one of these crying episodes but it was the first time she'd done it publicly and in front of Kaydence. Her crying spells seemed to *be growing increasingly intense but she kept it from everyone including her best friend. The relationship with Ernest was over but the pain laid active in her heart. She had been doing everything she could possibly think of to mask the painful experience. Partying and heavy drinking was her number one method of covering the pain. She did not want to revisit those memories of hurt.*

After what seemed like hours of crying they drove back to campus in silence. Delanie sat in a trance almost motionless. She could no longer hold her pain a secret. It had begun to interfere with her life. She was unsure of how to reveal the story of her life to her best friend who was practically a sister to her. Kaydence moved off campus the beginning of their junior year and although the two talked on the phone daily there was a decline in the amount of time they spent together socially. Finally, Kaydence mustered up the courage to ask Delanie what the crying was about. She listened actively as Delanie tried to explain. That was about three years ago.

Shaking her head in disbelief at the memory, Delanie

pulled into the parking lot. She was glad she took

Kaydence's advice and sought counseling. Delanie

stepped out of the car and gracefully walked into the

building to see Dr. Summers. The ever so cheerful

receptionist Sarah greeted her as she signed the

appointment book.

"Ms. McReynold, sorry Dr.Summers is running a little

late, she'll be here in about fifteen minutes. Please

take a seat. Is there anything I can get for you? Water,

coffee, anything?" Sarah stepped from behind her

desk.

"I'm fine, thank you. I'll just sit and flip through a few

magazines," she said taking a seat in the waiting area.

"By all means feel free," Sarah said.

The wait was shorter than expected. Dr. Summers

apologetically walked in.

"Delanie I'm so sorry for the wait. Please step into my

office," Dr. Summers lead the way. Delanie placed her bag on the couch, sitting down, she stared at the exquisite painting of waterfalls hanging on the bright yellow wall. Dr. Summers had strategically placed luxurious paintings of beaches, palm trees, and water falls on each corner of the walls. It was her way of inviting the "calmness" in as she puts it. This room which was once a strange sight to Delanie had now become a place of solace.

"You're looking good," Dr. Summers started with her usual compliments. "Now, where shall we begin?" She took out her note pad from her black leather brief case. "I've been thinking a lot about what you said about happiness and what it will mean to me? Truth is, I still haven't figured that out yet. I do however know that a lot of changes are happening."

"Great, let's start there," Dr. Summers said with pen in hand, ready to jot down notes.

Chapter
~Two~

Amigas

"Hurry up and get out here child, I don't have all day to be waiting on you," Delanie called out to Kaydence who was stuck in the bathroom creating what was sure to be a master piece of art. Kaydence could transform even the ugliest of duckling into a beautiful swan with mascara, foundation, eyebrow pencil, lipsticks, and a few brushes.

"Don't rush me. You know I gots to be cute!" Kaydence hollered back.

"We might as well go back to living together because you sure done took over my entire bathroom with all your make-up stuff," Delanie said walking over to the door way of the bathroom. She liked to watch Kaydence apply make-up although truthfully Kaydence did not quite need any make-up. Her caramel complexion was perfect without foundation. Delanie did enjoy viewing the finished products of Kaydence's work. Perhaps tonight she will let

Kaydence transform her face as well.

"I was just thinking about that the other day, I miss your crazy behind being all up in my space. Now it's payback," Kaydence laughed as she continued contouring.

"So where to tonight Ms. America?" Delanie asked viewing Kaydence's face through the mirror.

"I was thinking wings and drinks on South Street, what do you think?" Kaydence asked still working on her face. It will take about forty-five more minutes for Kaydence to be completely done.

"Yeah girl anything. I just want to celebrate," Delanie said leaning against the door frame.

"Woo woo! Twenty-eight!" Kaydence cheered.

"Twenty-eight and single and loving it," Delanie added.

"Well I don't know about the loving it part," Kaydence replied.

It was Kaydence's twenty-eighth birthday and for once she did not want to travel out of state to celebrate. It was going to be the two of them eating and laughing no girls trip just the two amigas.

"Remember when we were in high school and we said by twenty-five we were going to be married?" Delanie asked as she walked into the kitchen to get an apple off the table, she needed a snack to keep her mouth going so she wouldn't be much of a distraction to Kaydence or so she wouldn't get bored watching Kaydence apply make-up. Delanie didn't really want to know how to apply make-up, she had Kaydence for that. Besides make-up did not interest her all that much except for seeing it on Kaydence.

"Girl we were tripping, I was nowhere ready to be married three years ago, twenty-eight is young when you really think about, I just want to focus on my career and travel now," Kaydence said.

"Yeah I hear you," Delanie said biting down into the apple.

"So how do I look?" Kaydence asked turning away from

the mirror to face Delanie who was now back standing at the door way of the bathroom.

"Flawless! I'm telling you Kay, make-up is your thing. You should start promoting yourself on Facebook and Instagram. So many of these young girls out here doing it and making money, and some of their works are more scary than sexy but not you hunnii, you got it."

Kaydence looked like she should grace the cover of Ebony or Essence magazine.

Humbly Kaydence said "Aww thanks Dee. You really think so?"

"Girl yes! Trust me. I wouldn't lie."

Delanie thought of how some people use the term "friend" loosely but for her, after having so many people drop in and out of her life, she began to reconstruct her definition of the word friend. A friend to Delanie meant a non-judgmental person, loving and accepting of who you are. A person who does not exhibit jealousy toward you and one who gives encouragement. Someone who wants to see you succeed and does not compete with you. A person you choose to call family, a sister, and that is exactly who Kaydence was to her and had been for all these years.

Kaydence

This could not be real life. This is something you see on television or read about in the books somewhere. This is not something that happens to your best friend! Kaydence thought as she paced back and forth in her room. She shared a three bedroom off campus with two of her classmates. Thankfully they weren't home so Kaydence could scream and get all the cuss words out of her system.

" Girl, he better be lucky his fucking ass moved to New York or I would have broken his fucking neck!" Kaydence screamed. At first Kaydence was upset with Delanie for not telling her about the abuse. Then she

blamed herself for not being available to her friend as much as she should have. How did she not know that this was happening to Delanie? They were like sisters, she should have been able to spot those red flags. She wished Delanie would have told her sooner, before Ernest moved to New York.

Kaydence had zero tolerance for men who did not know how to behave like proper human beings. Her parents were married and she saw how nicely her father treated her mother. There had never been a day when he raised his voice at her mother let alone a finger. But Kaydence knew Delanie's story was different maybe that's why she tolerated that no good-not cute-sorry excuse of a man-crusty ass-boy child Ernest. Although several months had gone by since Kaydence learned of the abuse, she could not stop herself from getting angry every time she thought about it. Kaydence thought about what if that would have happened to her? Would she have been able to keep it a secret? She just could not imagine exactly what she would have done had it been her. The way her temper was set up, she probably would have been the one doing the abusing.

Now that everything was out in the open it was time to move on with life. She could tell Delanie did not really want or need to be reminded of those horrific events. What Delanie needed was empowerment and Kaydence had just the thing she knew would help.

"You know what I think Dee?" Kaydence said while turning on her HP.

"What you think Kay?"

"I think we should watch this vlog I found on YouTube the other day," Kaydence replied enthusiastically.

"Alright let me have a drink first," Delanie said.

"Sure thing," Kaydence said opening up her mini fridge in the room.

"All I have is liquor, liquor, and more liquor."

"I guess that'll do," Delanie laughed thankfully because she knew that alcohol usually had the opposite effect on

Kaydence. For some reason liquor always quieted

Kaydence down but she was fired up without it.

Delanie needed Kaydence to be calm.

"That's the spirit. No but for real though, I think you will

like this vlog," Kaydence excitingly said.

"Now I know you're not ready to seek counseling or

even start thinking about it but I think this vlog will help

you put things into perspective. This woman talks about

love, friendship, and not just romantic love but loving

yourself. Let's just watch," She did not want to push

Delanie to seek counseling just yet if she wasn't ready,

but she wanted to do something to help empower her

friend.

Kaydence smiled at the memory as she and Delanie

locked arms and walked towards the bar on South

Street. To say their college days were crazy would be

an understatement.

Here they were officially grown adults. Delanie had

turned twenty-eight three months back and now

Kaydence was turning twenty-eight.

"Girl you remember Same ol' lady G?" Kaydence asked as they approached the bouncers. South Street bar was the only bar she knew in Providence that had bouncers.

"How can I forget? You used to make me sit and watch those vlogs by force," Delanie teased thankful that Kaydence *did* make her watch those videos.

"Anyway girl that woman is making millions now. She is still on YouTube making vlogs. The other day I heard on the radio that she will be starring in some movie and she has a book coming out. It's crazy!"

"Wow!" Delanie said and made a mental note to google the book when she got home. Delanie didn't actually know why she stopped listening to SameolLadyG.

"Yes girl can you believe it?" Kaydence asked in amazement.

"Oh I believe it. She helped me a lot. She's very insightful," Delanie was not surprised that

SameolLadyG had written a book. She could not wait

to get her hands on that book. Perhaps it would help

her on this journey of rediscovering herself.

"I would love to meet her," Kaydence said as they sat

at the bar ready to place their drink orders.

"Me too," Delanie agreed then picked up her glass as

soon as the bartender handed her the drink. The

bartenders were usually quick with their drinks. She

and Kaydence were more like regulars at South Street.

"Let's make a toast," Delanie said raising up her glass.

"To being sexy, sassy, successful, and shit everything

else," Kaydence said laughing.

"Yes and to friendship," Delanie added.

Kaydence scanned the room and her eyes caught a

handful of eye candy. Kaydence appreciated the older

crowd that was drawn to South Street. Not those

young twenty something year old men-boys as she

referred to them.

"Girl the men in here are fine!" Kaydence said eyeing

this Lebron James look-alike brother. Then she quickly turned her face to Delanie before she ended up doing the unthinkable. Lord knows she did not have a shy bone in her body.

"Dee have you thought about dating again?" She asked trying to distract her mind off the Lebron look alike.

"Well, I thought about it but you know how I'm doing the whole celibacy thing. I guess for now I'll just have to live vicariously through you," Delanie replied.

"Live hunniii live!" Kaydence exclaimed. The truth is the thought of dating floated through Delanie's mind from time to time but falling in love was something she was not sure she was ready for just yet.

Tyson

"Turn with me to the book of 2 Timothy 4:7," Reverend Dr. Yasmin Lyman began addressing the congregation. "The title of my sermon is 'The fight for life' if you are there say amen and let's stand for the Scripture reading," she continued.

There is no other place Tyson Bailey would rather be on a Sunday than in church. It was a miracle that he had made it this far in life. At thirty-one years old he was just happy to be alive. According to man he should have been dead by now but God had kept him. Tyson was anxious to hear the word. He loved Reverend Yasmin's preaching. She was on fire for the Lord and there was no stopping her. He took out his Bible, a note pad, and pen. He was ready for his spirit to be fed.

"The enemy wants to keep you spiritually bonded. It is never about the physicality of things. Look beyond the physical and look at the spiritual. The devil will have you thinking that you will never die. That's why he entices you with physical things. He doesn't want you to know his tactics. He wants your spirit to stay here with him on earth that is why he offers you the world. The devil knows to stay on earth is eternal death, eternal torture and everlasting suffering. He knows there is no hope for him therefore he tries to steal, kill, and destroy you to keep you from reaching your destiny," Reverend Yasmin began her preaching, the congregation hollered a few "hallelujahs" and "amens" as she preached.

"Understand you were sent here on a mission from God. There is a purpose for your time spent here on earth. Your physical body is going to die but where you end up spiritually is what the enemy is fighting you for. Everything you encounter is preparation for your purpose. Look at every obstacle that comes your way as an opportunity to trust God. Do not be deceived, the battle has already been won. The devil was not sent to torture you but you were sent to torture the enemy. Don't give up your power. Don't be confused 'Greater is He that is in you than he that is within the world'. You are in a fight for life. Jesus said that "He has come so that you may have life and have it more

abundantly." Like Paul, let us fight the good fight,"
Reverend Yasmin continued her preaching. After about
an hour and half of preaching the service was over.
The rest of the congregation greeted one another and
"passed the peace."

Tyson walked over and hugged the petite framed
woman. "Reverend Yasmin, that was a good word,"
Tyson said greeting her.

"Thank you Brother Bailey. I'm just a messenger, a
vessel for the Lord sent here to do my job," she said
embracing him.

Tyson loved her humble spirit. Reverend Yasmin was
kind and sweet. All the years he'd been in this church,
dating back to his boyhood, he couldn't remember ever
seeing her angry. She had this 'tell it like it is' spirit
but did it so gracefully and with so much poise. Dr.
Samuel Lyman was a blessed man to be married to
such a wonderful woman. Tyson had his own parents
in his life but he looked to the Lyman's for spiritual

guidance.

"We are believing God to send you a young lady who can walk beside you as your wife. Trust me, my husband and I haven't stopped praying," Reverend Yasmin said as she got on her tippy-toes to place kisses on Tyson's cheeks.

Tyson smiled at her and said "Thanks Reverend, so am I."

In times past Tyson had strayed here and there not really focusing on the things of the Lord. He certainly had his share of a few crazy women. Tyson was not looking for a saint per say but he wanted and needed a woman who was serious about life.

"You know there are plenty young ladies right here in the church. You might not have to look far," Reverend Yasmin said interrupting his thoughts. He continued to smile at Reverend Yasmin and gave her a nod of agreement. There were a lot of beautiful single women in his church but truthfully Tyson viewed all of the women in the church as his sisters. He had grown too close to them and frankly wasn't attracted to any one of them in that way. Besides dating a sister in church usually complicated things and made things awkward. It was usually hard for them to keep their holier than thou persona especially after screwing, which usually resulted in an attitude towards him. Tyson recalled two sisters in particular who thankfully were no longer attending the church. Old habits are hard to break but with much help from the Lord and determination on his part, Tyson had recommitted his life to the Lord and so far he was doing great staying out of "trouble". The thought of marriage had surfaced many times on his mind. Many of his friends from college had already begun to marry and settle down with their wives and children except for him and his buddy Charles. Tyson believed God's time was the best and when that time approached he would know for sure, that was his prayer.

As Tyson drove home he thought about the direction of his life. He played back the sermon in his head and wondered what his purpose in life was. He was at peace with his life. Everything was not perfect but he at least had peace. He had a good job working as a Mechanical Engineer for a great company. He was heavily involved in the church choir ministry. Several people had told him on many occasion that his voice sounded a lot like R&B singer John Legend. Although he himself did not quite think so.

Tyson knew that the Lord never gives you more than you can bear. He was bearing his condition the best he knew how but he worried for the woman who God was going to place in his life as his wife. Lately Tyson had really begun praying for this mysterious woman who would keep him waiting at the altar. The thought made him smile as he entered into his black QX80 Infiniti. He blasted his favorite hip-hop gospel CD and drove out of the church parking lot.

Chapter

-Three-

Bondage

"Oh no please stop, it's hurting me, Ernest please stop!" Delanie struggled to get out from under Ernest's hot and sweaty body.

"Shut-up you know you like this shit, bend over, don't make me pull your fucking tracks out!" He screamed at her, forcing his manhood inside her.

"No! No! No!" Delanie screamed and jumped up in cold sweats. As she inhaled and exhaled heavily she managed to catch her breath from her horrible nightmare. She pulled her cell phone out from under her pillow case and looked at the time, 4:27am. An instant headache formed in her head as she hugged her pillow as tightly as she could. She got up, walked to the kitchen, poured herself a glass of cold water, then walked into the bathroom, opened the drawer and grabbed some pain relievers. *TGIF* Delanie thought as she headed back to her room and climbed in bed. She thought about switching on the television but there was not much to see on TV at this hour except for news shows, re-runs, and infomercials. It was too early to watch a movie or call Kaydence. There's no way she was going to fall back to sleep and wake up in the next three hours to prepare for work. *I'll just take a personal day* Delanie thought as she reached for her journal on her night stand. Delanie was determined to be set free from all things Ernest. She had become more aggressive about her freedom. Nothing was going to stand in her way, not even a nightmare. Delanie had found journaling, along with seeing Dr. Summers, to be quite helpful on her path to recovery. Staring at the blank page with pen in hand she wrote;

Dear Diary,

It is 4:29 AM and I just woke up from a nightmare. My head is pounding, sleep has left my eyes and all I really want to do is forget everything about Ernest. My mind is mentally a trap. This bondage is keeping my heart from opening up. I have taken all the necessary steps to getting my life back on track from watching vlogs to seeking therapy. Why isn't it working? What is really keeping me stuck in this state? Is it Ernest? Is it me? There is a lot to figure out but right now all I want to do is sleep. I want a way out of this mental bondage.

Delanie closed the journal, turned off the lights and decided to give sleep another try.

Changing Plans

As Kaydence poured the angel hair spaghetti out of the pot into the colander, steam rose up filling her kitchen. *Tonight is going to be a quiet night, spaghetti and meatballs for dinner and a little bit of TV* she thought. But before the thought settled into her mind her cell phone rang.

"Hey Girl," Kaydence said seeing Delanie's name on the screen.

"Hey hunnii what are doing?"

"Nothin' bout to eat this here spaghetti and meatballs I done prepared and call it an evening," Kaydence answered in an old southern woman accent.

Laughing Delanie said "Chile let's step out tonight. I had a long week at work and I need to get out this apartment for some fresh air."

"Come over let's hang here," Kaydence replied stirring the spaghetti.

"Nah I feel like getting dolled-up tonight," she said staring at herself in her full length mirror. She did not want to spend her Friday with sweats and a t-shirt on.

"Oh Lord don't get 'too too' dressed up now. I'll call Emily and see if she'd like to join us," Kaydence smirked as she poured the spaghetti onto a plate.

"Alright see you soon my love," Delanie replied.

"See ya," Kaydence replied.

Kaydence shook her head. *Only Delanie can make me change my plans* she thought to herself. Now what to wear on this chilly November night was her next struggle.

The ladies agreed to meet at "Whales" their favorite lounge for drinks. They looked stunning, rocking casual but sexy fall looks. Delanie wore blue distressed jeans that cuffed at her ankles with tan and black suede stilettos, a cream shear blouse with a tan blazer accompanied by an animal print scarf. Her beautiful natural curly afro sat perfectly on her head with gold hoop earrings. She finished her look with ruby red lipstick that complimented her Hershey brown skin. Delanie took Kaydence's advice not to get "too too" dressed up. Kaydence also wore a pair of blue jeans with black riding boots, a white blouse, and a black leather jacket. Her full jet black perfectly blow dried shoulder length hair looked great with diamond studs. She wore a nude color lipstick blending with her caramel complexion.

"Hey you look good," Kaydence said embracing
Delanie.

"So do you girl, where's Emily? Is she going to be able
to join us?"

Emily Campo was a mutual friend from high school.
Delanie and Kaydence loved hanging with her because
she had a no filter kind of mouth.

"Yes girl, she said she'll be meeting us here," Kaydence
answered.

The ladies walked in grabbed a table and began talking
while they waited for Emily to join them.

Fate

Now Tyson had his share of clubbing and lounges
days. Lately he only devoted his time to his career and
church. Charles, on the other hand, still had a lot of
clubbing left in him. Although he admired Tyson's new
life path, he was not quite ready to throw in the towels
to the night scene and give up the opportunity to

entertain the company of beautiful women. "God's not through with me yet," Charles often reminded Tyson as an excuse to continue his hunt for beautiful prey in any way he deemed necessary. Tyson was sure that tonight wouldn't be any different.

"I can't believe I allowed you to talk me into coming out tonight," Tyson said to his best friend Charles. Tyson was more of a home body. He did not like to go out much especially to these type of scenes and if there was ever a particular lady that caught his eye Tyson could think of many ways to entertain her without taking her to the club or a lounge. That was the old him and he just was not into that anymore. He hoped Charles would just allow him to chill the way he wanted to but that seemed to be a lost battle. Tyson wasn't overly religious or anything but he would just rather avoid temptation at all costs. He could not say for sure, but he highly doubted that the woman whom he'll choose to settle down with would be waiting for him at a club or a lounge.

"Oh come on Ty, it's no sin to be seen in a lounge. It's not like I'm asking you to have alcoholic drinks or anything, I just thought we can sit back and catch the game here," Charles said hoping Tyson would lighten up.

"We could have done that at the crib," Tyson said wondering why he always allowed Charles to talk him out of his plans even when he had his mind made up.

"Nah, ain't no chicks at the crib," Charles replied.

"Oh here we go," Tyson said smiling exposing his deep dimples.

 As they headed to grab a seat, Charles' eyes instantly caught Kaydence and Delanie sitting at a booth and he began to motion toward them.

"Where you going man?" Tyson asked already knowing the answer.

"To sit with those beautiful sisters over there," Charles said looking in Kaydence and Delanie's direction.

"We can't do that, what if they're waiting for their dates or something?" Tyson was amazed by how bold Charles had always been or maybe it was because he had been spending so much time in church that his perspective on life, love, and women had certainly change. He no longer looked at women as lustful creatures created to satisfy his sexual appetite. Whatever it was, he was sure oblivious to how things worked perhaps even rusty in the so called game of getting a woman's attention. In fact Tyson was not into playing any games at all.

"I doubt it," Charles added hoping Tyson would chill with this whole church boy attitude and relax a bit. Tyson could not believe he was walking with Charles to approach some sisters. It had been a while since he'd done this. He wasn't too sure what he'd say. Just then his eyes caught Delanie's and there was a magnetic pull that instantly drew him to her. Her beauty was radiant. She had the richest chocolate skin

he had ever seen. Suddenly his theory of not finding
the woman of his dreams waiting for him at some club
or lounge became just that, a theory.

"Hello ladies. I'm Charles and this is my buddy Tyson.
We notice you ladies have a great view of the television
and were wondering if you wouldn't mind us joining
you—"

"That is if you're not waiting for your dates," Tyson
added desperately hoping the answer would be 'no'.
Tyson was stunned those words actually escaped his
lips. He said a silent prayer in his heart. He had never
really felt this kind of attraction for a woman before. It
was not just her beauty although in his eyes her
beauty was equivalent to that of a goddess but he felt
as though his spirit recognized her spirit.

Delanie and Kaydence glanced at each other and
smiled.

"Actually a friend of ours is supposed to be joining us,"
Delanie spoke up taking a glance at Tyson. He was

strikingly handsome. Tall dark and handsome she noticed her heart beating fast as he spoke. His demeanor was different from his friend. He seemed shy, respectful, and polite.

"But she cancelled, so I guess it is okay for ya'll to join us," Kaydence added after catching the disappointing look that flashed across Tyson's face.

"Great!" Tyson exclaimed sounding a little too over joyed.

"It must be fate," Charles added as they sat down. Smiling Tyson said "Can we get you ladies another drink, food, anything for your generosity?" He kept his eyes glue to Delanie as he spoke. Tyson was glad that for once he had listened to Charles and agreed to leave the house. The night was just beginning and before it ended Tyson was determined to get Delanie's number. He had to see her again, this time *alone*.

Signs

So many clients come into my office looking for happiness, hoping there is something I can say to bring them to happy. How refreshing it is to know that Delanie is not just looking for happiness, she's choosing it Dr. Summers thought to herself as she drove to her office for another therapy session with Delanie. If there is anything she wants her clients to know, it's that happiness lies within them. She thought about how quickly change can happen in our lives, as humans we sometimes don't even realize that we are changing. Dr. Summers could see the changes that were happening in Delanie's life. Gradually she was on her path to finding happiness.

"So tell me about your new job. How are things going?" Dr. Summers asked.

"Things are fine. I have a case load of ten clients to assist with housing, child care, and other things but it's really good," Delanie answered getting comfortable on the couch.

"Great, I'm glad you're liking it," Dr. Summers said with her note pad in hand.

"Now let's talk about love. What are you going to do about love?" she held her pen ready to write.

"I don't think I can go there. Not right now," Delanie said. She was afraid to open her heart to anyone and frankly she wasn't quite sure she knew how.

"You know Delanie it's been a while since that relationship, since those events happened and you have made a lot of progress," Dr. Summers reminded her.

Delanie could not let this abuse continue to hold her back. She was now in her late-twenties and if she ever wanted to have the family she always dreamed of then she had to let go and start dating again.

"I know but I still don't understand why it happened to me. I don't understand why I allowed such a thing to happen to me. How could I have kept that a secret and continue going on as if nothing was happening?" Delanie questioned.

"Well..." Dr. Summers began.

"I mean I didn't see the change happening. I didn't see that this could be my life. It felt unreal to me," Delanie continued.

Delanie wanted to make those memories stop, no more nightmares or flash backs but the instant she let her eyes shut for a second, there they were again. She could picture the scene in her mind so vividly.

There he was knocking on her dorm room door. Excitingly Delanie opened the door. "What are you wearing?" Ernest said pushing past her to do his routine inspection of her outfit. Delanie had falsely mistaken this as a gesture of caring.

"Do you like it?" Delanie asked doing a little spin in her mini black dress.

"No it's way too short. Put pants on," he demanded. Avoiding an argument she sighed and looked through

her closet for a pair of low-riders blue jeans. She

convinced herself that he was just trying to protect her.

Ernest was a junior in College when Delanie was just a

freshman. He sought after her like prey and made

himself her boyfriend before she even knew it. Delanie

thought that she and Ernest were just friends initially

but in his sick twisted mind they were already

boyfriend and girlfriend and she belonged to him. Over

time he wooed her with his slick words of how she was

the most beautiful girl he had ever seen and a bunch of

other sweet nonsense. He certainly had a way with

words being a student of Mass Communication and all.

Delanie found herself spending practically every waking

second with Ernest. He always had a way of telling

Delanie what to do. "He's just firm. Our personalities

are a little different," She said to Kaydence along with

her other friends, making excuses for him.

She and Ernest were heading to the Union party to

dance the night away. The DJ played all the dancehall

reggae that Delanie loved. Whining and shaking to the beat she danced with Ernest and a few other guys who broke in while she and Ernest were dancing.

'What a fun night' she thought to herself as they walked back to her dorm room. She started to have small talks with Ernest but he stayed quiet the entire walk back. They entered the room and she took off her blouse, with just her bra and jeans on she motioned towards Ernest snapping her fingers dancing to the beat in her head. All of sudden he sent a fiery slap across her face instantly causing her to fall onto the bed with hot red liquid pouring out of her nose and into her hands.

"Don't you ever disrespect me like that," Ernest said calmly disregarding the blood that was profusely pouring out of her nose onto her chin, chest, and bed sheets. He walked out of the room slamming the door shut.

Completely in a daze Delanie laid on the bed with

blood all over her hands too confused to cry. What has just happened? She thought to herself. That was the first time Ernest had laid his hands on her.

Dr. Summers handed Delanie a box of Kleenex as tears were now streaming down her face.

"I don't know what made me stay in that relationship," she said bringing her focus back to present day.

"Sometimes we miss out on the signs and signals. What do you think some of the signs were that you might have missed?" Dr. Summers asked.

"His controlling ways, he also wanted to spend a lot of time with me. At first I thought it was cute. I thought that we were going through our honeymoon stage of the relationship and eventually he'd get sick of me but that didn't happen. He always wanted to know where I was. He knew my class schedule. He'll wait for me after class and walk me back to my dorm. Kaydence tried to tell me that Ernest was being possessive of me but I thought she was just being jealous. You know how a friend might typically react when one friend gets into a relationship. Plus she had just moved off campus and we didn't hang as much as we used to." Delanie sighed.

"When did you realize that your friend Kaydence was right about Ernest?" Dr. Summers asked handing Delanie more Kleenex.

"I guess I always knew she was right but I didn't want to admit it to her or better yet admit it to myself," Delanie replied exhaling. Enough was enough. She had to stop this entanglement.

"I want to explore a new me. That relationship with Ernest is over and has been for years. I don't even know why I'm still crying about it," Delanie said.

"It's okay to cry. It is part of your healing process." Dr. Summers assure her.

"Yes. I understand but I'm tired of crying over it. I'm sure he has moved on with his life. He got an internship with a radio company in New York, accepted a job offer and never looked back on me. It's like he didn't do anything. Like he never caused me any pain and abuse," she continued.

"So what is it that you want Delanie?" Dr. Summers asked.

"I want happiness. I want peace. I don't want to have moments like these any longer. I'm tired of being afraid of the events in my head," Delanie replied.

"What will make you happy?"

"I'm not quite sure but I sure would like to find out," Delanie answered firmly and she meant it.

"How do you want to go about finding your happiness?" Dr. Summers asked.

Delanie stared into blank space.

"I can't honestly say," she responded sadly.

"Okay then you have an assignment. I want you to write down one of the happiest moments in your life. Then I want you to think about what it is about that moment that made you happy. We will discuss your response next session. Can you do that?" Dr.

Summers asked.

"Yes I can do that. I'll get to thinking," Delanie

responded with a faint smile.

Chapter
~Four~

Small Steps

Delanie walked into work, cheerfully greeted her co-workers and sat at her cubicle. She turned on her computer to check her emails. There were four emails from the CEO of the company informing employees about the holiday party, an agency meeting, policy changes, and something else she couldn't remember. Nothing she needed to respond to. She pulled up her calendar and checked her itinerary for the day. She had three scheduled family visits. *Great I need to go for a ride.* She thought. Her mind had become consumed with thoughts of Tyson after their encounter at Whales. He was indeed very handsome man and quite humble unlike his friend Charles who was just too forward for her taste. Delanie felt a connection between she and Tyson but tried to resist it. She was by no means surprised when he asked her for her number so they could continue their insightful conversation. She smiled as she thought of how Tyson kept his eyes on her the whole night missing the entire football game. Delanie knew her mind was not ready to embark on getting to know anyone else but herself. Her therapy sessions with Dr. Summers had helped her a great deal but there were still a lot of healing that needed to be done on her part. That relationship with Ernest left a scar in her heart. Although her crying spells had stopped and she was trying her very best to get the pieces of her life back together, she still couldn't forgive herself for staying in an abusive relationship. She always wondered *what if Ernest did not get that internship and move to New York? Would they still be together? At what point was she going to walk away from that relationship?* She huffed. Delanie gave Ernest too much power over her all in the name of "love". Right now she was not interested in knowing so called love or even having sex which usually complicated things. She had been celibate going on two years now and was okay with her lifestyle until meeting Tyson. He woke up desire and urges that laid dormant inside of her. What she truly wanted was to heal her heart without any distraction. Shaking her head, she placed a phone call to her first family confirming their visit for the day. Delanie placed the other two calls to confirm the visits. She received two confirmations and one reschedule. She grabbed her bag with keys in hand and headed out of the building. Delanie made a mental note to stop by Dunkin Donuts for a medium strawberry Coolatta. Hopefully a sugar rush would boost her energy level and take her mind off Tyson.

Being a case worker opened Delanie's eyes to different perspectives on life. She had to admit she truly enjoyed working for Fresh Start. The families she worked with all had very interesting stories and life experiences. The more she helped them, the more she learned about herself. They inspired her without even knowing it.

Some families had been comfortable enough to share with her about what their lives were like growing up in Africa. Delanie could not imagine the hardships some of her clients had to endure, yet they were always kind to her, they were humble and happy. Delanie secretly wished she had half their strength. She was not quite where she would have liked to be in her life but she was also not where she used to be and for that Delanie was thankful.

It's a process she thought as she drove to her client's house.

Laughter

It's been months since Delanie and Kaydence hung out with Emily. "Girl I can't believe you stood us up last weekend. We met these two guys one was really feeling Delanie and the other I think you would have liked," Kaydence said.

The ladies sat at the food court in the mall playing catch up right before seeing a really hot romantic flick that everyone and their mama was buzzing about.

"Good thing I didn't come cause child I am so done with men," Emily said as she placed her purse on the table.

"What happen to the guy you were seeing the last time I bumped into you at Stop and Shop?" Delanie asked.

"Girl please, Ronald is a pathological liar," Emily said rolling her eyes.

 Delanie and Kaydence both looked at each other knowing that there was a drama filled story about to follow that statement. Thankfully they had about fifteen minutes before the movie started including previews and all.

"This fool had me believing he was single and what not. Girl we were kicking it like almost every night. He's coming to my place, I'm going to his. No sleep overs though, ya'll know I'm strict about that."

"Uh-huh." Delanie and Kaydence answered sarcastically in unison.

"So anyway, this one night while we were kicking it. It must have been about 1:30am or something. I hear keys rattling in his door. I'm looking at him and this man's not even flinching. So I ask him if he was hearing what I'm hearing. He had the nerve to play deaf. We're in the bedroom mind you and there's someone *else* who has entered the house and this man is not moving a muscle. I'm thinking to myself *what the hell is going on here?*" Emily said shaking her head in disbelief at the memory.

Kaydence and Delanie were both laughing hysterically with tears coming out of their eyes as Emily continued her story.

"In walks this fat chick. I called her fat Suzie, old girl snatch me out of the bed talking about 'bitch what are you doing laying with my man?' Now, ya'll know I ain't no punk so I swung at the bitch and we started going head up," Emily begin throwing up air punches reenacting the fight.

"Girl you got my side hurting," Delanie said holding on tightly to her stomach laughing uncontrollably.

"Ya'll laughing but this is no funny matter. That was the worst night of my life. Now I talk smack but I am not about that fighting life. Ronald put my life in danger then he had the nerve to say that was his psycho ex-girlfriend." Emily hissed her teeth in disgust.

"Ex-girlfriend?!" Kaydence and Delanie screamed in unison.

"Yes, ex-girlfriend chile, with a key to his place. Trust me when I tell ya, these men ain't about nothing. You can't trust them." Emily said matter-of-factly.

"Where do you find these brothers?" Kaydence asked still laughing hysterically.

"Girl I don't know. It must be my pretty face, small waist, and all that junk in the trunk that my mama gave me," Emily stood and turned showing off her figure.

The three of them laughed their way up the escalator to the cinema.

Back in her house Delanie thought about Emily's story and trust, she knew she was not ready to make herself vulnerable again. Her cell phone alerted her of a missed call and text message from Tyson while she was in the theatre. She contemplated calling him as she got undressed. A part of her wanted him to disappear out of her mind's eye but another part of her longed to hear the sound of his baritone voice again. Delanie laid on her bed with her phone in hand. "Urgh!" she grunted with frustration.

Chapter
-Five-

Life Questions

Kaydence was right. Same Ol' Lady G actually wrote a book which Delanie ordered off eBay. She sat at the kitchen table to read. *Can Same Ol' Lady G be any more brilliant?* She thought as she opened the book of poems.

What if we could write our own lives?

Will we skip hurt, regrets, and disappointments?

Will we skip the journey and jump to the outcome? How will we know what the outcome will be without the journey?

What if we could write our own lives, what would we say to ourselves?

Will we love ourselves enough to warn ourselves about the perils of life or will we just allow ourselves to figure it out?

What if we knew how our lives would end? Will we wait for

the ending or will we try to end it differently? If we change

the ending, did we really live our life?

Life will answer our questions of life.

"Hmm, those are interesting questions," Delanie said aloud.

Her phone alerted her of a text message from Tyson. She had completely forgotten to give him a call back. Suddenly the phone rang flashing his name.

"Hello," Delanie answered.

"Hey there beautiful I was beginning to think I had the wrong number," Tyson's baritone voice penetrated through her ears.

Delanie smiled with a hint of guilt. *He's too charming* she thought to herself.

"No, sorry about that I just— "she started to think of a lie to tell him.

"Hey no apologies necessary I'm glad you answered. How have you been?" Tyson asked.

"Comme ci Comme ca" Delanie responded. *Phew,* Delanie breathed, thankful she didn't have to tell him a lie. She began to doodle into the book.

"Oh okay. You speak French?" Tyson's sexy voice snapped her back into focus.

"Barely" she laughed, loving the sound of his voice in her ear.

"I'm surprised that you even know its French," Delanie said as she placed the cap back on the pen. She couldn't believe that she just doodled into the book. Tyson truly was a distraction. A very good distraction, one she didn't want to end.

"Yeah my French is probably as good as yours, if you don't mind me asking, why so-so? Why not great?" Tyson asked with so much concern. *Oh how sweet is he* Delanie thought. She loved the concern in his voice. They talked for about five minutes then Delanie had to quickly get him off the phone. The sound of his voice was sending electrical waves through her body. Something she was not too sure she might be ready for. Tyson seemed like a good guy but Delanie was skeptical of men. She had not dated anyone after Ernest. Although she wanted to "write her own life" as Same ol' lady G puts it, she had to figure out the direction in which she wanted it to go first. *No better time than the present though* she thought.

New

Tyson could not decide what to put on for his date with Delanie. Nervous and excited at the same time, he decided to go for a business casual look. He wore fitted Khaki pants with a blue and white plaid collar shirt and a V-neck cashmere sweater. Tyson wanted to do something other than the usual dinner date scenario so he chose an art bar in Boston for their first date.

"I have never been to an art bar. What's it like?"

Delanie asked sitting in the passenger seat looking amazingly stunning in her skinny leather pants with her beautiful taupe open knit draped sweater.

Tyson could barely keep his eyes focused on the road and the sound of her voice sent his heart beating double the normal beat.

"Well, according to the reviews it should be nice." This was also his first time going to an art bar. He wanted his first date with Delanie to be a new memory for him. He was pleased to hear that she too had never been to an art bar. Together they were creating new memories. Tyson wished to create a lot more new first time memories with Delanie and tonight was just the beginning.

"So you haven't been there either?" Delanie smiled.

"No, but I figured you might like it," Tyson said taking a quick glance at her.

"How you figure?" She asked with curiosity in her voice.

"Well since we met at Whales, I figured you like the lounge/bar atmosphere. You can have a glass of wine and showcase your artistic side on a canvas," Tyson responded.

"That sounds nice. Hopefully they have alternative drinks because I don't drink alcohol."

"Really, I just thought since you were at whales—"

"I must be a drinker?" Delanie interrupted.

"No—" Tyson could not believe how foolish and judgmental he sounded. He was truly trying to impress Delanie. He hoped that their night would not end up being a disaster.

"I'm sorry," he said hoping that he hadn't really offended her.

"It's okay. I used to drink but my weekly AA meetings require that I stay away from alcohol," Delanie replied with a straight face.

"Oh my God I had no idea," He said feeling like a complete 'A' hole.

Noticing the panic in his voice Delanie added, "I'm just joking." She chuckled and softly punched him on his arm. "Lighten up," she said smiling.

"Oh alright you got jokes I see," Tyson said. Oh how he longed to taste her lips. The way she smiled enticed him.

The two engaged in more small talk as they drove. Tyson was pleased with Delanie. He liked her sense of humor, in fact he liked everything about her. Their chemistry was in sync and Tyson could not wait to do this again. He was already planning their second date in his head and the third and the fourth and so forth. "I forgot how beautiful the city of Boston really is. I don't know why I'm always stuck in Rhode Island," Delanie said as they entered into the art bar. "Yes Boston is a beautiful city." Tyson agreed holding the door for her to walk in. "Oh thank you. You're such a gentleman." Delanie said seductively looking back at him. "My pleasure," Tyson blushed. The art bar was small but cozy. Canvases of many different paintings hung all around the room. There were mini easels with blank canvases on each table. The workers were extremely friendly. They greeted Tyson and Delanie when they walked in, and thanked them for choosing to spend their evening at the bar. They were informed about the complementary drinks on the house. Tyson and Delanie put on their aprons. "You look good with an apron on," Tyson said. Delanie smiled "Thank you so do you." They walked over to their seats. "I'm hungry. How about you?" Tyson said looking at the menu. "Well I'm not really hungry but I could eat," Delanie replied. "I like that. Why don't we order something then?" Tyson winked at her. "Sounds good to me," she picked up her menu and scanned through it. "I think I'll have a sandwich."

"I'm going to have a couple slices of pizza. I read that the food is really good here," Tyson said as he signaled for one of the employees to come over to them. They placed their order. "These paintings look like they were all done by professional artists. I'm not sure I even have a creative bone in my body." She looked at the display painting of what they were going to be imitating. "That looks really hard. I'm not sure I can do that," Delanie said nervously. "Oh don't be nervous I'm sure they're going to walk us through the process," Tyson assured her. "You think?" Delanie asked. "I hope so," Tyson said examining the different paint brushes. Delanie laughed at him. She could see nervousness all in his face. The food came along with the complementary drinks. "Oh perfect timing." Delanie said, as she received the food. She held up her glass. "What shall we toast to?"

"Well let's see, to a fun night of creativity and to new experiences," Tyson said holding up his glass to meet hers. "Hmmm I don't know much about the creativity part but I'll drink to that." They toasted and waited for the instructor to begin showing them how to create a masterpiece of their own.

Happiness

Happiness is a state of mind. One must make a choice to pursue it regardless of circumstances and situations. I have found that true happiness which leads to pure joy does not stem from within yourself alone but from a being more powerful than you. As for me it is my faith and belief in Jesus which has brought me to pure joy. My belief in something beyond me is what keeps me sane. I have realized that often times we look to others to bring us happiness but what we fail to realize is that others are also looking for happiness.

Delanie listened to Tyson's voice play back in her head as she hung her painting on the wall in her living room. To her surprise the painting came out better than she imagined it would. She could not believe how much fun she had with Tyson. Her experience at the art bar was amazing. A sense of happiness crept into her spirit. *This is what life should be about,* she thought to herself.

What a level headed, kind, sweet, and insightful man Tyson is, plus a man of God on top of it all, Delanie smiled as she thought about Tyson.

She tried to remember the last time she was in church. As a child she grew up in the church but as she got older and life began to happen to her, she found herself slipping out of the church.

"Maybe that's what's missing in my life," Delanie said to herself out loud.

She had to admit that she had become spiritually disconnected and also emotionally destroyed. Delanie was fighting an internal battle. She wondered if she was truly ready for this thing with Tyson. She did not want to end up somehow ruining his life. However, she was certainly glad to have met Tyson. Delanie sat on the couch and stared at the painting she created on the wall. Tyson and her were beginning to create memories together. Delanie wondered what it would be like to hang more memories on the wall, especially on a wall in a home with Tyson. She blushed at the thought. "It is way too soon to be thinking about that," she said aloud. It had been a long time since she thought about marriage or a relationship with any guy. It was always something she wanted, something she dreamed of. Perhaps that was part of the reason she stayed with Ernest. She shook her head 'no' at the thought of Ernest. She did not want him to rob her of this moment of bliss especially now that she was learning to love her life and to cultivate some happiness of her own.

The next day Delanie went to see Dr. Summers.

"I met a guy," Delanie told Dr. Summers on the couch. She was anxious to tell Dr. Summer's about her date with Tyson.

"Great! Are you seeing him?"

"We went on our first date. At first I was uncertain, but

I'm glad I went. He said something about happiness that really got me thinking." Delanie shared Tyson's philosophy with Dr. Summers.

"That's wonderful. Speaking of happiness did you complete your assignment?"

"I did. In fact after my date with Tyson was when I really began to think about the happiest moment of my life. I must say it had to be the day I graduated college," Delanie said.

"Okay. Let's explore that. What was it about that moment that made you so happy?"

Delanie exhaled as she thought of the best way to formulate and speak her thoughts.

"It was not so much about earning my degree. For me it was about my perseverance and ability to go on after the abuse with Ernest. I buried myself in my books when he left for New York. I blocked out every moment of abuse and focused on finishing what I came to do in college,"

Dr. Summers listened attentively and took notes.

"Do you think you have that same ability now?"

"What the ability to be happy?" Delanie asked.

"I was speaking about perseverance but yes. Do you think you have the ability to be happy?"

Dr. Summers questioned Delanie smiling knowing that she was on the verge of her breakthrough.

"Yes not only do I have the ability to be happy, I have the power to be happy as well."

"That is awesome!" Dr. Summers exclaimed extremely proud of Delanie.

"Now that you have this knowledge what do you plan to do Delanie?"

"I plan to live out my happiness," she replied.

Chapter

-Six-

Dating

Tyson was intrigued by Delanie's story. The more he got to know this woman the more he loved her. She was without a doubt a virtuous woman. He felt honored that God made it possible for the two of them to cross paths. Tyson was determined to make Delanie his wife. Getting to know Delanie had been the best decision he'd made in a long time. Her laughter was electric, her transparency was rare and her wisdom was empowering. Tyson was truly glad she chose to reveal a part of herself to him. Over their last dinner date Delanie revealed to him how she lost both of her parents before the age of ten and grew up being raised by her aunt. Tyson could not relate to what it would have been like to lose a parent. His parents were all he had and he was extremely grateful to God for them, especially for his mother. Given his condition, no other woman could take care of him like his mother had done but Tyson wished and prayed that God would give Delanie the strength to handle his condition.

Tyson looked at the clock, it was 8pm. He had prepared himself for this moment, eliminating all distractions. Now it was time for him and Delanie to engage in their nightly talks. "Getting deep" was what they called it. Delanie always had something profound for them to discuss. He was eager to find out what the topic would be for the night. Tyson headed to the living room, sat comfortably on the couch and dialed Delanie's number.

"Hey there young lady, how are you?" He said ready to engross himself to the sweet sound of her voice.

"I'm good young man ready to get deep? Delanie asked, laying comfortably on her bed.

"You know it," Tyson responded with enthusiasm.

"Wonderful. So what's our topic for tonight?" She asked.

"I was hoping you had one," he laughed. Tyson enjoyed the conversations he and Delanie had about dating. He had to admit that it was nice to not only date but to talk about it as well. He loved listening to her perspective on the topics of dating.

"Not tonight sweetheart. I had a really long day at work and honestly I was looking forward to you enlightening me about life," she said smiling.

Tyson loved hearing the word "sweetheart" flow from her voice into his ears.

"I guess you leave me no choice then sweetheart," he jokingly replied.

"Let's talk about the number one killer of relationships. I think it is communication or lack of communication. What do you think?" Tyson asked.

Delanie usually had a contradicting response to whatever it was Tyson said, but that is what he enjoyed most about their conversations.

"I think communication is important but my question is why is it the number one killer of relationships?" Delanie asked.

"Because it is hard."

"You know what, I don't think communication is hard," Delanie said.

"Really you don't think so?" Tyson replied not at all surprised at her response.

"No, I don't, to me communication isn't hard at all. It is the willingness to communicate that is hard."

"Hmm, enlighten me," Tyson said. Delanie certainly had a way of shifting his thinking.

"Communication itself is an ongoing process of talking, listening, reflecting, analyzing, and interpreting. The process is not hard however it is time consuming. The willingness to engage in such process is where the challenge lies for most couples. And personally I don't think men do well with that process," Delanie stated. Tyson laughed at her last comment.

"That is deep you're right communication is a process but it's not that men don't do well with the process. We just do the process differently from women." he added.

"I can agree with that. Maybe we just need to understand what each other's method of processing is," Delanie said. She could literally spend all night talking to Tyson.

"Exactly, we sure do," Tyson agreed as his deep voice flowed through the phone causing all kinds of reactions inside of Delanie's body.

Tyson could also feel his temperature rising and his blood flowing extremely fast through his veins as he and Delanie continued their conversation.

Girl Talk

"You know I was thinking with the summer approaching we should plan an all-girls trip. Go somewhere fun...that is if you're not too wrapped up with Mr. Tyson."

"Is that jealousy I hear poking its ugly head through your voice?" Delanie teased.

"Girl please that church going brother ain't got nothing

on me. I am your sister from another mister," Kaydence answered.

"Well there is this one thing he has that you don't have," Delanie said.

"Okay Ms. Nasty. Giving up celibacy I see."

"Nah but it's tempting. Extremely tempting."

"I don't know how you do it girl because the brother is fine!!!" Kaydence said.

"I'm truly trying to fix me Kay and you know sex complicates things. Thankfully I don't have to worry about that because Tyson is also saving himself."

"Saving himself? Is he a virgin?" Kaydence asked as she pulled the bag of popcorn out of the microwave.

"Child no. Trust me, I asked. He's also practicing celibacy, trying to stay on the straight and narrow unlike your devilish self."

"Girl pray for me now that you're into church and what not. I tell ya something certainly got into me last night," Kaydence said.

"Something or someone?" Delanie asked.

"Sit, sit, sit I got details."

"Oh Lord. I might as well live vicariously through you seeing as how I might not be getting any until God knows when," Delanie said as she took her spot on the couch next to Kaydence.

There was never a dull moment whenever Kaydence and Delanie got together for their weekly girls night. Tonight they decided to stay in at Delanie's place. They ordered pizza, popped some popcorn, put on a romantic comedy and talked.

Kaydence filled Delanie in on her latest rendezvous with a co-worker while Delanie talked about how things were going with her and Tyson. The ladies enjoyed the night with laughter and the best pizza Rhode Island had to offer.

After cleaning her kitchen and putting the trash out, Delanie stared at the outfit Kaydence helped her put together for her surprise date with Tyson. Once again

Ms. Fashion fanatic had certainly come through. The simple yet elegant all-purpose black dress was perfect for any occasion. Delanie did not even realize she had such a dress in her closet had it not been for Kaydence keen sense of fashion.

Courage

Sometimes in life one just has to take a bold step and do something out of the ordinary Tyson thought. Sneaky was not really his style of doing things but when Kaydence number popped up on Delanie's phone while she was using the restroom at his house, he took a glance at the number on the screen and stored it mentally before handing the phone to Delanie. It had been six months now and Delanie was still being a little iffy about introducing him to her friends and family. Tyson wished she would give him the opportunity to meet the people who were important to her. Other than their original meeting at Whales,

Tyson had not seen Kaydence since, although Delanie was always on the phone talking and texting when the two of them were on a date. He didn't sweat it though. Tyson's love for Delanie was growing at an increasing rate and he wanted her to be as comfortable as she could be whenever she was around him.

Tyson could not understand how Delanie could be so free and joyful around him filling his ears with laughter and his mind with insightful thoughts, yet so guarded when it came to her family and friends. He was ready to let Delanie meet his folks right after their second date but she insisted that she needed more time to see how their relationship progressed. Six months is enough time Tyson figured. He was ready to do what he was about to do but he needed help. Thankfully Kaydence was really understanding after much convincing and explanation of course.

Tyson felt really bad for putting Kaydence in that predicament. Delanie and Kaydence were thick as thieves. He truly admired the love they had for each other. It was as if they both shared a womb. It certainly would be a challenge for Kaydence, but he was certain it was a challenge she would be able to accomplish. Besides, desperate times called for desperate measures.

Chapter
-Seven-

Kairos

"This looks like a church building. Tyson what are we doing at the church?" Delanie asked as Tyson opened the car door for her to step out.

"Well there is a special event going on tonight," He said.

"What kind of event? Tyson you should have told me we were coming to church."

"It's after church hours so technically—"

"It's still a church building and I'm dressed inappropriately," she said staring down at her six-inch stilettos.

"You look fine, no one is going to judge you. This is church remember," Tyson said grasping her hand.

"I do, which is why I'm really nervous."

They walked into the sanctuary which was set up like a five star restaurant with white linen cloths on round tables accompanied by crystal vase center-pieces.

Exactly what kind of special event is this? Delanie

thought.

"A special guest is joining us tonight for the event that's why the sanctuary is set-up the way it is," Tyson answered as if he read her mind.

"That must be a really special person."

"Yes very special indeed. Now come meet my family."

They walked hand in hand as Tyson approached an elderly couple.

"Mom, Dad, this is Delanie."

"Oh Delanie we are so excited to finally meet you!" Mrs. Bailey said hugging Delanie tightly. There had been talks about Delanie meeting Tyson's family but she imagined it would be in a more intimate setting like their house perhaps.

She did not imagine that Tyson was referring to his actual family.

Not realizing he was referring to his actual family, she glanced at them in astonishment and whispered to Tyson. *"I thought you were talking about your church family. I did not think your parents would be here."*

"Yes they are here for the event also. I figured this would be a great way for you to meet my church family as well as my biological family," Tyson said with a smirk.

Delanie enjoyed the warm embraces of Tyson's parents especially his mother. Mrs. Bailey hardly wanted to let go of Delanie.

"When will this event start?" Delanie asked.

"Shortly, let's take our seats. Reverend Yasmin should be addressing the congregation soon." Tyson said.

They sat and engaged in small talk with Tyson's parents. Everyone seemed overjoyed to have Delanie in their midst. They were all so very kind and welcoming to her. Just like Tyson predicted, Reverend Yasmin came up to the pulpit and greeted the congregation.

"Welcome everyone, it is great to be in the house of the Lord. Tonight is indeed a night of celebration. We have with us a very special guest but before we can introduce our guest I would like to call on brother Tyson to come on up here. I believe he has a selection for our guest. Let's welcome him," Reverend Yasmin stated.

Delanie was aware that Tyson sang with the church praise and worship team but she had never actually heard him sing. *What a sweet surprise* she thought, applauding him with the rest of the congregation as he approached the microphone.

"Before I begin my selection I would like to call up someone who is very near and dear to our guest. Without further a due I would like that person to please come up."

Everyone looked around as a woman holding up what seemed to be about one hundred red roses to her face walked up to the pulpit.

"Now I had the pleasure of meeting our guest of honor nearly six months ago. Today it is my pleasure to present to her these roses along with this—" Tyson stated.

Delanie gasped as the woman holding the roses slowly let it down exposing her face and handed Tyson a box. Barely able to stand to her feet Delanie rushed out the door before Tyson could begin his speech. Instantly dropping the mic Tyson chased after her.

"Delanie wait!" Kaydence called after her as she followed Tyson running down from the pulpit.

"I can't believe you did all of this. And Kaydence, ooooh I'm going to kill you two." Delanie grunted with embarrassment.

"It was supposed to be a surprise. One I thought you would like," Tyson said.

"Oh but you thought wrong. I am not ready for this. I want to go home," Delanie said panting.

"Why because you're afraid?" Tyson asked nervously.

"Afraid? It's been—"

"Six months, I know," Tyson said.

"Yes, most people wait a year or two sometimes three,"

Delanie said panting.

"Well I can't wait another day. I don't have two or three years," Tyson replied.

"What?" Delanie asked surprisingly.

"What I'm saying is... I knew I wanted to marry you the moment I laid eyes on you. And yes some men wait two or three years but I'm the kind of man who believes in going after what he wants the moment he sees it," Tyson said falling down on one knee.

"Now I know you're scared but so am I. There's a lot that we do not know about each other but we can learn. So standing here outside the house of the Lord although I wish it could be inside, Delanie Savannah McReynolds, in front of the house of the Lord with my family, pastors and friends present, will you marry me?"

"Tyson, I wish you would have told me then I wouldn't have worn this tight dress. I'm humiliated," Delanie replied.

Tyson laughed "Then it wouldn't have been a surprise."

"Hey I picked out that dress," Kaydence added.

"Yes I know and for that you will pay," Delanie said smiling.

With tear-filled eyes, she looked at Tyson on bended knees, stretched out her left hand and gave her answer. Everyone cheered.

"Now let's go in so you can hear your selection," Tyson said scooping her off the ground.

Prep

"I thought you were my sister from another mister, my ride or die but you sure done crossed over becoming best buds with Tyson and keeping secrets from me," Delanie teased.

"You took the ring didn't you?" Kaydence teased back.

"I sure did!" Delanie answered staring at her two carat princess cut engagement ring which sat perfectly on her finger.

"It is gorgeous!" Kaydence exclaimed.

"You know it practically killed me having to keep this secret from you. And the way the man begged I just could not say no."

"I know you got a weakness for men who beg," Delanie winked.

"Uh-huh and I know how stubborn you are. You would not have agreed for Tyson to do this if I hinted it to you. So I had to keep my lips sealed."

"Yeah you right. You know me too well."

"Let this man love you Dee. I see the way you glow at the mere mention of his name."

"But don't you think it's too soon?"

"Of course not."

"But what if I haven't fully healed?" Delanie asked truly concern about her past interrupting her future.

"You just deal honey. As you deal you'll heal. You can't put your life on hold," Kaydence said.

Delanie knew Kaydence was right. She could not afford to let fear poke its' ugly head out so she quickly pushed it back in with faith.

"He proposed to me. He proposed with a diamond ring," Kaydence began singing as she walked over and place her arms around Delanie.

"Shut up child. I really should slap you for that stunt you pulled with that dress knowing damn well he was going to propose in a church," Delanie said half joking.

"I told you, you needed to spice up your wardrobe. You're welcome. I know Tyson appreciated it," Kaydence said laughing as she sat back in her seat.

"I don't know what to do with you except pray," Delanie said shaking her head.

"You do that and let me sing. We're getting married we're getting married!" Kaydence continue in her so singing pleasing voice.

"Shut up Kay. You know how this world is set up. People are going to think I'm actually marrying your crazy behind," Delanie teased.

"I don't care what people think. I'm ecstatic," Kaydence could not believe was about to get married. She was so excited that Delanie decide to open heart and love again.

"Ok Ms. Ecstatic. I am going to need all your help Madame Maid of Honor A.K.A wedding planner," Delanie said getting back to business. She did not want to lose focus.

"Please don't be a bridezilla," Kaydence teased playfully rolling her eyes.

"Oh you haven't seen nothing yet. I plan to work your last nerve," Delanie teased back.

"Okay let's get serious. What do you need me to do?" Kaydence asked ready to assume her role as the maid of honor.

"Girl, everything! There's so much to do from picking a venue, to dress shopping, cake tasting, to premarital counseling. I don't know where to start," Delanie sighed.

"Well let's start by placing our order with this fine young waiter. Lord knows I'm starving," Kaydence said.

Reverend Yasmin

Much to Delanie's surprise, her family really took a liking to Tyson, especially her aunt Helen who raised her. Although her family was unaware of the engagement, they were thrilled for her. Aunt Helen made Tyson promise to redo the proposal along with an engagement party. He happily agreed and offered her family his sincere apology. They accepted.

"You can't put a time limit on love baby," Delanie could hear Aunt Helen's voice play back in her mind as she got dressed for their premarital counseling session with Reverend Yasmin. It was customary in Tyson's church for engaged couples to participate in premarital counseling. An overwhelming thought of excitement flowed through her mind as she thought of how

different life was about to become. Delanie was truly glad to have Kaydence, Aunt Helen, and Emily to help her with all the planning stuff, but most importantly she was glad to have Tyson for helping to fill her heart with love. Dating without having sex was quite interesting and fulfilling, she wondered why in the heck she did not remain a virgin before marriage. *'One last counseling session with Dr. Summers is a must'* Delanie thought. Dr. Summers has without a doubt helped her battle her past demons. She had to share this great news with her. "Thank God for counseling," Delanie said as she grabbed her keys and drove to the church.

Looking handsome as always, Tyson greeted Delanie with soft wet kisses to her lips.

"You look beautiful," he said.

"Thanks. You're not half bad yourself."

Tyson laughed as they walked into the church.

"Here comes the happy couple. See the Lord does

answer prayers Brother Tyson," Reverend Yasmin said

embracing them.

"He sure does Reverend," Tyson agreed.

Delanie blushed with a mixture of shyness and

excitement enveloping her face.

"Are you two ready to talk marriage business?"

Tyson looked directly at Delanie with love beaming

through his eyes.

"Yes," they both answered.

"Well then join me in my office, shall you?"

Being familiar with counseling was good but

counseling with the Reverend would probably be a lot

different from what Delanie was used to. She

wondered what exactly they would talk about first.

Finances? Communication? Sex? How to pray as a

family?

Oh boy, do I have to keep my statements, comments,

and questions holy, she thought.

Smiling, she intertwined fingers with Tyson's and they

walked up the stairs into Reverend Yasmin's office.

"Please have a seat. Would you guys like some water, macadamia nuts or saltine crackers? Which is about all I have here in my little office. Don't judge," Reverend Yasmin said.

"Water is fine please," Delanie said smiling.

"Don't be shy now sister Delanie. We're family now."

"I'll take water as well."

"Oh now this 'two becoming one' thing should be easy for ya'll," Reverend Yasmin teased as she grabbed her snack basket, placed it in front of them along with two bottles of water from her mini refrigerator.

"Please help yourselves to some snacks when needed. An hour is a long time."

Reverend Yasmin took her seat behind her desk.

"I know I don't have to say this to the two of you but I will say it anyway. Marriage is not for children. It is serious business. My husband and I have been married for twenty-one years and it is *hard,* even for

me and I'm close to perfect need I remind you,"
Reverend Yasmin said jokingly.

Tyson and Delanie both laughed loudly.

"I think we're ready aren't we sweetheart?" Tyson said,
placing a kiss on Delanie's cheek.

"Alright now ease up on all that kissing. Save if for the
honeymoon, ya'll know there is no sex before marriage.
You two have to honor each other and honor the Lord."

"Yes Ma'am," Delanie said.

"Sex is an important element of marriage. The best if
you ask me," Reverend Yasmin said.

"Oh my goodness," Delanie said chuckling. She could
not believe how down to earth Reverend Yasmin was,
not like those old stuffy preachers. She was beginning
to see why Tyson loved this church so much and was
always raving about Reverend Yasmin.

"Yes girl. We are getting straight into it. That's how I
like to do it. Skip the small talk," Reverend Yasmin
replied.

Delanie could not stop grinning with anxiety.

"This should be fun," Tyson added.

Flies

"Over my years of being a Reverend I had the privilege of counseling quite a few couples before they took the step into marriage. This is a calling I am truly honored to have bestowed upon my life, but I must admit my heart aches when I hear and see some of those couples who unfortunately were not able to commit to their vows," Reverend Yasmin fixed her glasses on her face as she stared directly at Tyson and Delanie.

"Now brother Tyson and sister Delanie I want you both to know that marriage is not just a commitment but it is a covenant between the two of you and God. Do ya'll understand what I mean by that?"

"Yes Ma'am," both responded.

"Now we have all heard the saying that communication is important in any relationship, especially in a marriage. Being married for a little over two decades, I would have to agree with that statement," Reverend Yasmin smiled.

"Oh by the way feel free to interrupt me anytime if any of you have a question or comment."

Tyson looked at Delanie.

"I'm just so glad that you agreed to do this for us Reverend," Tyson said.

"Oh of course! This is a dream come true, not just for you, brother Tyson. You know how much my husband and I have been looking forward to this moment. In fact I was getting ready to set up a profile for you on one of those dating websites. The Christian ones of course."

Delanie burst out laughing, "Reverend Yasmin you truly crack me up."

"Wait till you hear her sermons. You won't know what to do with yourself," Tyson added.

"Well you know laughter is good for the soul they say."

"Yes it is," Delanie agreed. Her mind was filled with

amazement as she intertwined her fingers back into Tyson's.

"Let me tell ya'll a story. I remember back home, I grew up in Jamaica. When I was a little girl I used to watch people eat outside. My mother never allowed my siblings and I to eat our food outside. We had to eat in the house. Anyway, sometimes I would see people leave their food unattended to go back in their house for something. Almost always whenever the person returned, their food would be infested with flies and it was no longer good for consumption. But if the person never left their food to go back into the house for water or something, I would watch them wave away the flies as they came near the food. But for those whose food was infested with flies, I'd watch them throw the food away in anger. Now I used to think to myself, it is not the flies fault for entering into unattended food," Reverend Yasmin paused and took a sip of water.

"This is the same concept with marriage. If you leave

your marriage unattended it becomes open to the public and someone or anyone can come and play in it. In this day and age do not leave your marriage open to social media so that "friends" or "followers" can enter into it. Keep your personal business off the internet. People stand by waiting, speculating, and definitely hating. Guard and protect your marriage. Do not give way to the 'flies'. Be attentive and drive them away as they come."

Chapter
- Eight -

Twilight Zone

"Dating is fun but dating your fiancé! Girl what is that like?" Kaydence asked Delanie as she applied make-up on her face helping her get ready for her date with Tyson.

"It's all still brand-new Kay. Honestly I'm trying to process it but the excitement is too much for me to even stop and think," Delanie said, looking up at the ceiling as Kaydence attached the false lashes onto her eye lashes.

"I am happy for you Dee. Tyson is a great guy."

"He truly is Kay. I love how he stimulates my mind and keeps me laughing."

"Uh-huh I bet you can't wait for him to stimulate other parts of your body," Kaydence teased.

"Oh stop it little Miss Nasty. Hurry up with this make-up child. I don't want to keep the man waiting on me the entire night."

"Almost done hunnii. Remember you can't rush

perfection. Where are you guys going again?"

"He said he wants us to try this Asian restaurant down town. The scenery is spectacular, it has a great view of the city."

"Oh yeah I heard the food is great too. You guys will have an amazing night," Kaydence gathered her make-up items and began packing up to leave.

"Call me when you get back home. I want to hear all about it. Don't you try to leave out any details either," Kaydence winked.

"Alright I won't. What are you getting into tonight?" Delanie asked.

"Nothing much. I'll probably look through my little black book and see who I can invite over to keep me company for the night."

"Oh my goodness, I don't even want to know," Delanie walked Kaydence to the door. They embraced each other.

"Have fun Dee."

"Thanks Kay. I'll call you," Delanie said closing the door. She quickly grabbed her cell phone and text Tyson, "on my way".

Arriving at the restaurant Delanie handed the valet her keys. It was quite chilly for a May night. The temperature had made a drastic drop which was so common in Rhode Island. She put on her blazer and stepped out of the car. *I hope he has not been waiting too long,* she thought as the hostess greeted her at the door.

"Reservation for two under the name Bailey," Delanie told the hostess.

"Yes Ms. McReynold, Mr. Bailey is expecting you. He called and said he will be about ten minutes late. Right this way. I'll seat you, and your waitress should be with you shortly."

Delanie could not believe that after all that time it took her to get dressed Tyson was not already at the restaurant waiting for her. She wondered why he didn't just text or call her instead of calling the restaurant. *Then again he's probably trying to be extra romantic and mysterious*, Delanie thought. She placed an order of a glass of wine and soaked in the beautiful view of the restaurant. She felt a little awkward sitting alone. *He better get here as soon as possible if he knows what's good for him*, Delanie thought. Fiancé or no fiancé, she was not about to wait on any man. Almost half way through the glass of wine she pulled out her cell phone; still no message or missed called from Tyson. "Where are you? I'm getting ready to leave," she texted and waited for another five minutes. Delanie got up walked to the ladies room and called Tyson.

"Hi you've reached Tyson Bailey I'm unable_" Delanie hung up on the voice mail.

"I can't believe this, I'm leaving," Delanie said aloud. She walked backed to her table signaled for the waitress to come over.

Delanie could literally feel the tightening of her skin as the biggest frown formed on her face. She sped off quickly, as soon as the valet handed back her keys.

"Forty-Five fucking minutes! I sat for forty-five fucking minutes!" she screamed into the cell phone.

"Wait what happened?" Kaydence asked perplexed.

"I got stood up Kay! That's what the fuck happened!"

"Calm down Dee. There has to be an explanation. Have you tried calling him?"

"He's not answering, urgh! I don't know if I should be angry, worried, or cryyyy," Delanie said, beginning to sob.

"This is not real life. I don't know what's happening."

"Dee I'm sure there is a reason for this, just drive over to my place." Kaydence said trying to calm her down.

An instant migraine formed from the million and one thoughts that were rushing through her head. She was foaming with anger. *I am going to KILL Tyson*, Delanie thought as she drove to Kaydence's place.

Trial

"I would hate to involve his parents because he's not a kid but I swear to God. He has the next hour to get in touch with me or I'm calling his parents," Delanie said sitting at the kitchen table with Kaydence.

"Let's just wait and see what happens. I'm sure he will get in touch with you before the night is over." As soon as Kaydence finished speaking, Delanie's phone rang with Tyson's name flashing on the screen.

"Answer it Dee."

"I can't, I want to cuss Tyson the fuck out! You answer it."

"Hello Tyson," Kaydence said.

"Hi Kaydence. I know she's upset but can you put her on the phone please?"

"Tyson I don't think—"

"Please Kay I need to explain something to her," Tyson pleaded. Kaydence could hear the faintness in his voice. She muted the phone.

"Dee he wants to talk to you. I think something happened," rolling her eyes Delanie took the phone from Kaydence.

"What is it Tyson? What the hell happened to you?"

"Dee I want to see you, can you come see me?" Tyson said.

"Come see you? Tyson what the hell is going on? You had me waiting in that restaurant for freaking forty-five minutes like a fool!"

"I'm at the hospital Dee."

"What?!" Delanie's heart dropped. "Are you okay? What happened?" She asked panicking.

"I'll be fine but I need to see you. You can come with Kaydence. My Parents and Charles are here also. I don't really want to say this over the phone. Please if you can, just come."

"Tyson tell me what is going on. Please I'm shaking right now," Delanie said pacing back and forth.

"I swear I will explain everything to you as soon as you

get here. Let Kaydence drive please. I got to go the doctors are coming," He gave her the room number and quickly hung up.

"He's in the hospital," Delanie said staring back at Kaydence with astonishment.

"Let's go," Kaydence said grabbing her keys. They rushed to Rhode Island hospital with quickness.

Chapter
-Nine-

Truth

"Hey there young lady. Thank you for coming. Kaydence, thank you for bringing her," Tyson said.

Delanie felt nausea. She wanted to puke. She hated the smell of hospitals. It always gave her a sick feeling.

"No problem. How are you?" Kaydence asked.

"Hey I'm fine," he replied nonchalantly sitting up in the bed.

"I'm used to this. Mom, Dad, Charles, Kaydence, can I please have a minute with Delanie," Tyson added as he sat up in the bed. His mother glanced over at him with the, *you should have told her a long time ago look in her eyes.* He glanced back at his mother with a look that said, "I know."

"Come sit next to me," Tyson patted the bed and made room for Delanie.

"We're not married yet. We can't be in the same bed," she said with her hands folded across her chest as she stood. She did not honestly feel like sitting down. She was too anxious and wanted to know what was going on with him. "Oh that's right I forgot, almost though. That is if you still want to marry me after I tell you this," Tyson said smiling. Delanie did not want to engage in small talk. *What the hell was he about to tell her?* She thought with a perplexing look on her face. Tyson exhaled, held her hand and stared into her eyes. "I wanted to tell you Dee from the moment I met you. The thing is... I wasn't sure how to say it. Truthfully speaking it was selfish of me to not tell you. I just did not want to lose you," Tyson paused. He was struggling with how he was going to reveal his condition to Delanie. He needed her to understand his reasoning for keeping it a secret. "You see the thing is Dee..." He continued as Delanie listened attentively without moving a muscle.

"I had a crises on my way to meet up with you. Charles was over at my place. He drove me to the ER and called my parents. This was after I called the restaurant and told them to inform you that I would be about ten minutes late."

"A crisis? What kind of crisis?" Delanie asked.

"No, not a crisis; a crises. A pain crises. I have sickle cell Dee." Silence filled the room as she stared at him. Delanie could not muster up the next word to say.

"The reason I kept it from you is because of my past experience with revealing it to women. Some of the women I've dated in the past, once I revealed to them that I have sickle cell anemia, they either stay out of pity or leave abruptly after. I know it was selfish of me to keep it a secret from you but I could not stand the thought of losing you," Tyson sighed, as he studied her face for a reaction. "Are you upset?" He asked. As a matter of fact this news had sent anger through her heart.

"I'm so upset I want to___"

"Kill me? Sickle cell is already doing that," Tyson said, trying to make light of the situation. He could see the tension in her face. She softly punched his arm.

"That's not funny Ty and don't think I won't kick your

butt because there are doctors and nurses around,"

Delanie said almost smiling. She couldn't believe that

Tyson was cracking jokes at a time such as this.

"You're always trying to kick my butt," he laughed.

"No but seriously Tyson I'm not upset that you have

sickle cell. I am upset that you kept it from me and

kept it this long. I mean we are about to get married.

We have talks about everything else and for you to feel

like this is not something you could have told me, it is

hurtful." Delanie did not want to appear insensitive,

she could not help but wonder about his level of trust

for her.

"Did you think that marrying me would be a guarantee

that I would not walk out on you? I mean c'mon

Tyson...we're going through premarital counseling for

goodness sake. We've been talking about trust,

honesty—"

"You're right. I'm sorry Dee. I apologize," Tyson interrupted. He was unsure whether or not she would still want to go through with the wedding. "So what does this mean Tyson? Did you really think I was not capable of loving you through your condition?" Delanie loved Tyson with every fiber of her being. He had entered into her life and freed her heart from all things that reminded her of Ernest. She would never think of walking out on him but she still did not think that it was fair for him to keep this from her. Delanie did not know much about sickle cell, other than it was a blood disease that affected mostly African-Americans.

"It's a lot to handle Dee and honestly as much as I cannot stand the thought of losing you, I completely understand if you no longer want to go through with the wedding," he finished his statement with so much sadness in his voice.

"I love you Tyson. I give you my word that I will marry you. You're in luck because I am a woman of my word, but no more secrets."

"No more secrets I swear," he said gazing into her eyes.

"So can you tell me a little bit about sickle cell and what it means?"

"It means that I'm in pain. Every now and then I'm in chronic pain. It's a blood disorder. Not contagious but it can be inherited. So if we have children there's a possibility they could have it based on your test. If you have one abnormal hemoglobin gene which means you will have the trait and not the disorder itself like I do then yes our children can possibly have sickle cell." Tyson paused and looked at Delanie. She looked very confused.

"I know it is a lot and it's confusing. You can ask me any question you have about it and I will explain it to you best I can for you to understand. Later we can talk to the doctors for more clarity and understanding. I'm really sorry Delanie that I kept this from you."

"I understand why you did it Ty. You don't have to

keep apologizing. How painful is it babe, if you don't mind me asking?"

"It's extremely painful but you know what, I don't allow it to stop me from living and I don't want to start now," Tyson answered. He pulled her closer to him and whispered in her ears. *"I love you Delanie and I cannot imagine my life without you in it. Please forgive me for withholding this from you."*

She held his face and kissed him long and hard. "I'm not going anywhere Tyson. I love you too baby, in spite of this condition. Thank you for sharing this with me, and yes I forgive you."

Bended Knees

Delanie fumbled through her purse for her keys, inserted the key into the keyhole and opened her apartment door. She raised her purse over her head and swung it on the couch. Paper, cell phone, and every other item fell out of it. Delanie glanced at the items as they hit the floor. She did not bother to pick

them up. She felt the wall for the light switch, flipped
it on and began to strip out of her clothes. Her
perfectly perky breast stood firmly on her chest, with
just her black laced panties as she walked into the
bathroom. She slid open the shower curtain kneeled
before the bathtub and turned on the water. The
sound of the water pouring heavily served as a
distraction to the thoughts in her head. Delanie placed
her right hand over her forehead and felt her skin. It
was hot. She was definitely getting a fever. Her head
hurt. Since Tyson had been in the hospital, she had
not slept for three days. She turned off the water, took
the stopper from the drainage and allowed the water to
run through the drain. She walked out of the
bathroom into her bedroom plopped her body onto her
crisp white comforter. Delanie laid on her back and
stared at the ceiling. Her bed did not provide her
comfort. She worried about Tyson. She thought, how
could she possibly rest when the man whom she loved

dearly was lying in a hospital bed? Delanie continued to stare at the ceiling not wanting to think or feel anything but she felt it all. The pain crept from the depth of her stomach. Her chest tightened with intensiveness. She turned her body around and lay on her stomach. Burying her head in the pillow, she let out a loud cry. Delanie screamed and cried until her throat began to feel sore. The ringing of her cellphone intercepted her cry. She stopped screaming but continued to sob as the cellphone rang. *Whoever it is, will stop calling,* she thought, but the phone continued to ring, with frustration she rose from the bed and walked back into the living room. She searched through the pile of things on the floor to find the phone that would not stop ringing. "Hello," she answered in a hoarse voice.

"Hey there young lady. How you doing?" Tyson's voice quickly filled her face with a smile. Delanie held the phone tight to her ears and breathed slowly. She cleared her throat in hopes to disguise the shakiness of her voice. "Hey babe. I'm okay. How are doing?" she replied wiping the left over tears off her face. "Better than yesterday. I should be getting out of here soon. I miss you Dee." Sniffling she replied, "I miss you too babe rest up. I will stop by later to see you." She did not want him to detect the sadness that was slowly creeping through her voice. "Alright young lady. See you soon and Dee—" Tyson paused. "What is it babe?" Delanie asked anxiously. "I don't want you to cry, everything is going to be okay." Tyson always had a way of knowing when something was not right with her. "My allergies are acting up babe but I'll come see you as soon as I can. I love you Tyson." "I love you too Dee and like I said baby, don't cry and don't worry everything is okay," She chuckled a little. This was one of the many reasons Delanie had fallen so deeply in love with Tyson. He was completely selfless, given the predicament he was in, he still cared for her well-being. They hung up the phone and she kneeled down in front of the couch folded her hands in a clasping stance and prayed. Delanie had not knelt down to pray in years. Right now more than ever she needed a miracle. She needed God. She closed her eyes and let out the words, "Please Jehovah if you can hear me, please Lord don't take Tyson away from me. Heal him Lord, I know you are a God that does miracles. God please! I love that man, please heal him Lord." For twenty minutes she stayed on her knees repeating the words, "Heal him Lord."

Bravery

Tyson was flipping through channels when Delanie entered into the room. "Hey young lady. You look beautiful," he said taking his eyes off the TV. Delanie blushed. She loved how Tyson always thought she looked beautiful even when she was wearing sweatpants and sneakers. "Thanks babe, what are you watching?" She said as she took a seat on the bed.

"Nothing much just flipping through channels," he handed her the remote to choose what she wanted to watch. "Naw babe I don't care to watch TV," she said taking off her sneakers to lay in the bed with him. "You just can't wait to get in bed with me, can you?" He teased. "Oh please you know you love it, push over," she placed her head on his chest and sniffed the hospital garment he was wearing. "Gosh you smell awful Ty," she said half-jokingly. "Ha! You got jokes but seriously I can't wait to get out of here and take a decent shower," Tyson held her tight and planted kisses on her cheeks. His kisses relaxed her. He stroked his hand through her hair as she listened to the rhythm of his heart beat. Her eye lids grew heavy and slowly shut on her. "Dee wake up. We're good to go," Tyson said softly tapping her outer thighs. "Huh," she said trying to open her eyes. She had fallen deep in sleep and completely forgotten where she was. She opened her eyes and looked up at Tyson who was fully dressed holding his discharge papers in his hands.

"What time is it?" she yawned. "A little after 3PM. My

parents are expecting us. You good to drive or should I

drive?" Delanie sat up and stretched her arms. "I can't

believe I fell asleep," Delanie said.

"You were tired. How you feeling?" Tyson asked

admiring her beauty. "My throat is a little dry." He

poured some ice water into the plastic cup and handed

it to her. She guzzled down the water. "I'm a little

embarrassed. I'm supposed to be the one taking care

of you and here you are taking care of me," Delanie

said yawning.

"Oh please girl don't even worry about it," Tyson said

as he bent over to kiss her. Delanie groaned inwardly

with the touch of his wet kisses on her lips. They

continued kissing for what seemed like eternity.

"I better stop. You're making want to stay in this

hospital bed for another hour," Tyson said fighting

hard to keep his lips off her lips. He grabbed her purse

and handed it to her as she put her sneakers back on.

"You ready?" he asked holding her hands as she stood

to her feet. The way Tyson was treating her you would

think she was the one that had just gotten discharged

from the hospital. "So you good to drive or should I

drive," he asked again. "I can drive babe," Delanie said

wishing they were already married. God only knew the

things she would have done to him in this hospital

room. She smiled at the sexual thoughts that were

running through her head. Those kisses really had her

hot and bothered. "So what did the doctors say?"

Delanie asked. "Everything looks good, I was given

some prescription to help with the pain but right now I

feel fine," Tyson said not wanting her to worry much

about him. Delanie felt a sense of release holding

Tyson's hands as they walked out of the hospital

together. She could not wait to be his wife. She

admired his bravery, knowing he was trying to remain

strong for her. His words said that he was fine but she

knew that he needed some time for recovery. Delanie

planned to be by his side every step of the way.

Chapter -Ten-

A Mother's Love

"Hey look, here come the soon to be newlyweds," Mrs.

Bailey hollered to Tyson and Delanie as they

approached the door steps.

With all that was happening Delanie had not been able

to focus on the wedding planning. Thankfully

Kaydence and Emily stepped in and took charge of

running after the small but necessary details.

"Hey no love for me?" Tyson said while his mother was

still embracing Delanie. Mrs. Bailey was beyond

grateful that God had sent Delanie into Tyson's life.

"Oh come here son, my big baby," releasing Delanie

from her tight embrace, she wrapped Tyson in a huge

hug as he placed a kiss on her cheeks. "How you

feeling son?" She pulled her arms from around him to

look at his face. "I'm good Ma just need to take a

shower and wash this hospital smell off of me."

"Well come on in, your father is in the living room

watching television." Mr. Bailey was a kind, gentle

man with a monotone voice. In all of Tyson's life he had never seen his father display an ounce of worry. Mr. Bailey always appeared content and happy with life no matter what was going on. Mrs. Bailey on the other hand was a worry wort. Tyson was thankful for the comfort, support, protection, and love his father provided for their family. His father gave balance to his mother and Tyson wished he could do all of the things he had seen his father do for his mother, for Delanie. Tyson's one goal was to consistently fill Delanie's heart with happiness regardless of what it would take him. Tyson needed to be at his parent's house for a few days until he fully recovered and could return to work. He knew his mother would give him enough TLC to get him through the next few days. Tyson was not ashamed to admit that he was indeed a Mama's boy. Delanie sat on the couch next to Mr. Bailey while Tyson freshened up in the bathroom. "You like the history channel?" Mr. Bailey asked without taking his eyes off the TV. "Yeah it's fine," she said viewing the side of Mr. Bailey's face. Tyson was a splitting image of his father. Mr. Bailey was a sneak peak of how Tyson would look when he's gray and old. Delanie smiled at the image of she and Tyson growing old together sitting in rocking chairs on the balcony of their southern home. Delanie had thought about moving to the south a few times. Once she and Tyson were married and settled, after a few years she would love to move to the south, preferably Georgia. The warmer weather would be great for Tyson. There would be less chances of the cold triggering a crises for him. "Delanie come in here baby," Mrs. Bailey's voice interrupted her thoughts of the future. Delanie got up and walked to Mrs. Bailey who was standing in the doorway of the bedroom.

"Leave that old man alone, us girls need to talk," Mrs. Bailey said gently holding Delanie's hand. The table was set and they were waiting on Tyson to finish showering so they could eat dinner.

"Let me show you something before Tyson gets out of the shower and tries to stop me," Mrs. Bailey said pulling open her night stand drawer. "Go ahead sit down," she said to Delanie, noticing the hesitation on her face. "It's okay. You can sit. I'll sit next to you," Mrs. Bailey said. They sat on the bed. Mrs. Bailey opened the enormous family album. "You're the first girl Tyson has ever brought into our home," Mrs. Baily said giving Delanie a pleasing smile.

"Really?" Delanie asked shocked and flattered at the same time.

"Yes. He told me about one or two girls he was dating in his early twenties. Nothing serious of course," Mrs. Bailey said with a wink. "I used to worry about him you know. I asked him why he wasn't getting serious with anyone. He told me 'Ma I don't want to put any woman through what you're going through with me' That broke my heart. I used to pray day and night that

God would send him a woman who would love him and stick by his side. I want to grow old knowing that my son has a wife and children of his own. I want him to experience the kind of love that his father and I have. I want to see my grandchildren. The thought that sickle cell was robbing him of all of that angered me to my core," Mrs. Bailey sighed heavily, turned the album page and revealed a baby picture of her holding Tyson. Delanie smiled at how adorable Tyson was as a baby. "How are you doing baby? How are you holding up?" Mrs. Bailey asked Delanie before turning the page again. Delanie took a deep breath and said "Well...I'm trying my best to process it all but honestly—

I want to know, how you deal with it Mrs. Bailey because I cannot stop crying. I'm angry too that he has to go through this and I feel so helpless."

Rubbing Delanie's hands Mrs. Bailey said, "When I gave birth to Tyson that was the happiest moment of my life. I loved how his little fingers would grab on to my index finger so firmly. I loved the smell of him. He was a happy little baby. He did not fuss at all and would only cry if he was hungry. Once I fed him he would go back to being happy and playful again. Tyson did not cry even when his diapers were wet but one night I heard a strange cry coming from my baby. I rushed to his crib and picked him up to find his hands and feet swollen. I immediately woke his father up and we drove to the emergency room. Since that night, since the doctors informed us that my baby had sickle cell anemia, I have spent countless hours in and out of the hospital, emergency rooms, and intensive care units. I have watched my son cry uncontrollably in pain. The doctors had given him thousands of medication. He has gotten blood transfusions, gone through surgery, but yet the pain kept returning."

Tears began to well up in her eyes; her voice grew shaky. "Oh Mrs. Bailey I'm so—"

"It's alright," Mrs. Bailey said, wiping the tear drop

that had fallen down her cheek.

"When I fell in love with Tyson's father we did not think about no condition, blood disorder, or diseases. We just loved. We did not know that we were both carrying traits of sickle cell until we gave birth to Tyson." Delanie made a mental note to call her doctor's office and schedule a blood test immediately. "You asked me how I deal," Mrs. Bailey's voice continued. "I just love. As a mother, there is no feeling in the world worse than watching your child suffer in pain. I know all about feeling helpless and defeated Delanie. Believe me I know that this is a lot to handle. Over and over again I have blamed myself *and* his father *and* God for giving our baby a tainted blood. It is unfair that Tyson has to go through this but all I can do is love him through his pain. As he's gotten older he's experienced less and less crises but I tell you, each time I get that call that he's in the hospital, each time I have to see my son laying in a hospital bed, it breaks me into pieces. I can tell you really love Tyson and I want you to know that he—" the knock on the door interrupted her sentence.

"Hey Ma we're starving out here," Tyson said slowly opening the door. He let himself in and his eyes quickly met the family album on his mother's lap. "Oh my goodness. I can't believe you're showing her those embarrassing pictures of me. Please Ma put that away." "I have seen it all," Delanie said teasing. She was glad that Tyson walked into the room and released the heavy sadness that was beginning to form in her heart.

Chapter

- Eleven -

Voices

Delanie needed to come to terms with the fact that Tyson had sickle cell. Tyson did not display self-pity and he certainly did not want Delanie to pity him. That was easy for him to say and do. He had lived with the disease for thirty plus years, Delanie thought. She hadn't even known the disease for three months. She desperately wanted to honor Tyson's request of not displaying pity towards him. Delanie tried hard not to allow pity to color her face in the presence of him but the truth is she felt sorry for him. She *did* pity him. It bothered her that he was sick. It bothered her that he had to battle a genetic disease, something he didn't choose and had no control over. Delanie settled into her house. She put on some comfortable gray sweatpants and turned on her laptop, she wanted to do more research on the disease and gain some more understanding of how others were living with it. She opened the YouTube app and typed in "living with sickle cell." Many videos popped up with females as the spokesperson. Delanie was glad because she needed to hear the rare truth of the reality of living with sickle cell. Before clicking on any of the videos she made a mental note to send Tyson a text message reminding him to rest up and take his medication. If they were married, Tyson would have been right in the bed room as she sat at the kitchen table in front of the computer. The thought made her smile. Tyson and Delanie had both decided not to cohabit before the wedding, specifically because of their religious beliefs. Since meeting and dating Tyson, along with the recent event of sickle cell becoming the fore front of her reality, Delanie had made an effort to develop a relationship with God. She prayed all the time, mostly for Tyson, and she was even attending church again. Delanie pulled out her cell phone and wrote the text. "Hey baby, I'm home. I had a great time with your parents. Please rest up and remember to take your medication sweetheart. I love you. Talk to you soon."

She pressed send. A minute later she glanced back at

the phone, no response from Tyson. He's probably

deep in sleep, if not he would have responded in

seconds, she thought, knowing him too well. He

usually responded to her messages within seconds

unless he was sleeping or in the shower. Delanie was

glad that Tyson had his parents to take care of him. A

bit of sadness came in her heart as she wished she

hadn't lost both of her parents. Aunt Helen was great

though and had been an amazing mother to her.

Thoughts of Aunt Helen lifted her spirit as she pressed

play on one of the videos. The woman in the video

spoke about her challenges of living with sickle cell

and raising her daughter. That video was empowering,

then she watched several other videos after that. The

raw truth that these women displayed in the videos

were extremely disheartening and sad for Delanie to

watch. She cried through several of the videos as she

listened to the voices of people living and dealing with sickle cell. One woman spoke about how she was in denial when the doctors first told her the news that her baby daughter had sickle cell. Delanie watched the lady cry and sob throughout the video as she explained her struggle with raising a child with sickle cell. That video in particular made her think of Mrs. Bailey and how strong of a woman she was, but more importantly how strong of a person Tyson was to endure such agony and pain and yet still remain positive. Delanie must have watched about twenty videos or so. She listened to every word that every single person said about their struggle with the disease. She could feel their pain as the tears rolled down their faces. Delanie cried heavily with some of the people as if they were sitting right before her. Their faces and voices were different but their stories were the same. Sickle cell caused them great unbearable pain. Many times they had to face their own death.

The disease had disrupted their lives over and over again. Hospitals had become like a second home to them due to many admissions. IV fluids, surgeries, and taking constant medication was their reality and hope for managing the disease along with watching their diet and staying away from germs to avoid infections. How can these people remain strong? How do they not break down through such heavy pain? They all seemed like super humans to her. Tyson seemed superhuman to her. To endure such adversity and remain hopeful was truly remarkable. Delanie too felt hopeful that she could love Tyson through his condition. There might not be much that she could do about the fact that Tyson had sickle cell but she could do plenty to not allow sickle cell to have her joy and stand in her way of marrying the man she loved.

Celebrate

The days and nights seemed to be growing shorter as the time of their wedding approached. It was exactly two weeks before their special day and Tyson could feel himself embracing the changes and letting go of all of his anxiety. He was more than ready to embark on a life journey with Delanie. He and Delanie decided to take one day out of the week to go on a date and escape the pressures and stress of wedding planning. Date night had become something Tyson looked forward to, especially tonight. For the first time Delanie would be entering into his house, a house that would soon become a home for both of them. They had agreed to move into his two-bedroom town house after the wedding. Right now Tyson's house was simply a bachelor pad and more so of a man cave. He had all the necessities he needed to live but there was not much style or design on the inside. However, tonight he went above and beyond to make sure the place would be pleasing to Delanie's eyes. Delanie received the results of her blood test which called for celebrating. They needed a safe and intimate place to discuss family planning. Tyson was beyond ecstatic that she did not have sickle cell trait. Now there was no chance of their child or children inheriting the disease only a chance of possibly becoming a carrier of the trait. That was something Tyson could live with as long as his children never have to endure the pain of sickle cell. The thought of having children with Delanie excited him. He could not wait to exchange life-long vows with the woman who had not only captured his heart but every other organ within his body. He checked on the bottle of Sauvignon Blanc wine which sat perfectly in the wine cooler chilling on ice. Tyson opened the cupboard and took out the wine decanter along with two tall wine glasses and placed it on the dining room table. Fresh blood-red rose petals lay on the floor marking the way from the front door into the dinner room. Tyson would do anything to make sure Delanie felt like the queen that she was to him. The beam of car lights flashing through the living room window indicated that the love of his life had just pulled into the drive way. Tyson quickly walked into his room and sprayed some cologne before heading to the door to let her in.

Love Grows

This was the best salmon, rice, and collard greens Delanie had ever tasted. Tyson truly was a man of many talents. She was in awe of how much work and effort Tyson put into making their date night beautiful. The home cooked meal, fresh rose petals, wine, and soft R&B music playing in the background were all too perfect and amazing.

"Baby the food was delicious! How'd you learn to cook like that?" Delanie asked, scraping off the last grain of rice from her plate with the fork.

"My mom taught me. Since I am her only child, she made sure I knew how to do everything. I also think she wanted me to learn how to cook to give her a break from the kitchen. She always used to say that cooking

for my father and I was like cooking for children living

on the missionary. That's how much food we ate.

Delanie laughed imagining the sound of Mrs. Bailey's

voice saying that statement. "Well I am thankful she

did teach you how to cook because you know you will

be giving *me* a break from the kitchen," she teased.

Delanie actually enjoyed cooking. Preparing meals

brought out her creativity and much joy. At one point

in her life she did consider attending culinary school to

learn more about the art of cooking.

"I plan to," Tyson said, as he got up from his seat,

walked over to Delanie and kissed her softly on her

lips.

"Hmmm, your kisses taste better than your meal,"

Delanie said loving the feel of his lips pressed against

hers.

"Don't tell me that or I just might spend all night

kissing you," Tyson said smiling. He kneeled before

her, gently wrapped his arms around her waist while she sat in the chair. Delanie lower her head and placed her hands on his cheeks. The two of them were face to face staring deeply into each other eyes. *"Please do. I promise I won't stop you,"* Delanie spoke in a soft whisper-like voice. Tyson could feel the blood rushing through his veins. It was only of matter of seconds before other areas of his body started to swell. Standing to his feet he said "It's getting hot in here young lady, why don't we go for a walk?" Delanie stood up as well, thankful that he said something. Honestly the decision to remain celibate until the wedding was becoming harder and harder with each second that they spent alone together. The temptation to touch him in places that are hidden through clothes were all Delanie could think off. Tyson held her hands and helped her to her feet. "Let's take a walk in the park," He said as they walked to the front door. "Well aren't you just Mr. Romantic?" Delanie teased. Tyson smiled and placed his hands in hers as they headed out the door. The warm summer breeze greeted their skin. "Wow it is gorgeous out here tonight," Delanie said inhaling and exhaling summer's air. "It is and the park is only about a ten minute walk from here," Tyson said. He was glad that the fresh air was releasing the growth of his precious vessel between his legs. They strolled hand in hand into the neighborhood park. There was a bench underneath an oak tree where they sat. Delanie had never really stopped to look at the stars at night. How tiny they appeared so far away in the sky, but shining so bright. The warm summer breeze felt great as it blew her hair into her face.

"Babe I want to ask you something," she said to him immediately after they sat down.

"What is it sweetheart?" Tyson asked.

"You know how I just love to hear your perspective on things...?" Delanie shifted to face him.

"Yes I know and for that I'm glad," he chuckled.

"Well yes. Let's get deep real quick."

"Okay let's do it," Tyson anxiously replied.

"How does love start?" She said with a straight face.

Tyson looked puzzled.

"Okay let me rephrase it. How did you start to fall in love with me?"

Tyson breathed easily and wiped the strain of hair that was blown in her face by the wind.

"I'll answer both questions. Honestly speaking, you don't start with love. No one starts with love. You start with wanting to love. You start with the desire to love. Overtime love grows, love develops. Love is a choice. The desire, urge, and courage to intentionally care for someone other than yourself is how love begins. I had that desire before I met you. The moment that I set my eyes on you and listened to your voice, was when I decided to act on my desire. I purposed in my heart that I was going to love you and I do love you." Tyson stopped talking when he felt her tear drops on his hands. Softly he kissed each drop of tears off of her face. He spoke quietly into her ears. "I love you Delanie and I am literally counting down the days to become your husband. You are the best thing that ever happened to me. I love everything about you and I mean that from the bottom of my heart."

Chapter
-Twelve-

On the Couch

It was a pleasant surprise to run into Dr. Summers at the grocery store. Delanie had been meaning to call her and set up an appointment. Delanie felt like she needed one more confessional session with Dr. Summers especially now that the wedding was only days away. What Delanie had been feeling could be passed off as a typical bride-to-be experiencing cold feet, however she needed the solace of Dr. Summers' office so that she could exhale. Stepping out of the elevator she signed as she walked through the lobby into the reception area. Dr. Summers welcomed Delanie in and she sat down on the ever so familiar couch.

"My, do you look like a bride to be! You are absolutely glowing! Are you excited?" Delanie had given Dr. Summers some brief information concerning the wedding the day they ran into each other at the grocery store. But there were more pressing issues which had lead Delanie to see Dr. Summers, for what she hoped would be the last time. Delanie needed to voice the thoughts and feelings that were tangled up inside her head and heart. Exhaling Delanie responded, "I am, but I'm also afraid that he will leave me." A puzzled looked appeared on Dr. Summer's face. "Leave you, how?"

"Well not intentionally I hope, a part of me wants to quiet my thoughts, I want to stay hopeful but I can't lie to myself. These thoughts consume me, it is all I think about. I really want to enjoy him. Enjoy every moment of our life together but I feel like I can't." Her voice began to crack. "You can't?" asked Dr. Summers. Delanie took a hard swallow of air into her lungs, "I can't because I don't feel right. I don't feel like its right to pretend that this doesn't—I mean isn't a reality. But I don't think it's right to also dwell on it but I can't help it Dr. Summers. I can't! Tyson is sick! And I don't know how long I am going to have him in my life," She exhale as tears flowed down her eyes. Dr. Summers handed her a box of tissues.

"I can't believe in just literally three days I will be Mrs. Tyson Bailey and I don't know how to feel," she let out a soft chuckle.

"How do you want to feel?" Dr. Summers asked.

"I want to feel excited, I want to feel ready, I want to feel beautiful, I want to feel loved!" She said smiling and cringing her hands in excitement. Then Delanie folded her hands together and looked to the floor. She spoke in a whisper like tone. "I don't want to feel afraid. Why do I feel like I'm always going to be afraid? Like it's not ever going to go away?"

"Why do you think you feel that way Delanie?"

In a regular tone voice she spoke up. "Partly because of his condition; partly because of my past experience but mostly because—mostly because, I think—I think no one completely gets free of fear. We get free of certain fears and then we create different fears. It's just something we create. Fear, because life without fear is fearful! Like who doesn't have it? Who doesn't have fear? Is it *even normal to* not have fear? You have to have some form, a little bit, *something.* That's part of life."

Dr. Summers smiled at her as she finished her statement.

Wedding Bells

So many details go into wedding planning, thankfully all of the small details were adding up. To say that Kaydence and Emily had been amazing would be an understatement. Delanie stared and unzipped the dry cleaner's bag that held her wedding dress. Before her very eyes hung her gorgeous fit and flare, sweetheart neckline, Ivory wedding gown with exquisite intricate pearl and rhinestone beading around the waist. Delanie choose Ivory because she believed that only virgins should wear white on their wedding day and since she was far from being a virgin, Ivory was the next best thing. She did however decide to cover her face with a veil which Tyson would have to lift up and unveil her during the ceremony. *"Actually the real unveiling would happen during the honeymoon night,"* Delanie thought to herself smiling. She pinned the long cathedral veil into her hair and watched it flow down onto the rug. "Everything will be perfect," she told herself staring into the full length mirror. Delanie pulled open the wedding book that she created along with Kaydence and looked over the details one last time. It read: Cocktail 6-7pm. First dance, toast, cutting of the cake, dance with parents/guardians, 80 RSVP received. Ceremony- 2:30pm at Loving Christ Church in Providence, RI. Tyson and groomsmen get dressed at Aunt Helen's house, eat breakfast, and get into the limo at 1:30pm. Bride and Bridesmaids get dressed and do make-up at the hotel downtown. Ceremony officiated by Reverend, Dr. Yasmin Lyman.

Traditional vows, reception hours 6-9pm, then party.

Menu: chicken cordon bleu and seafood stuffed sole,

mushroom risotto. Cake: carrot cake with caramel

filling, and lemon cake with lemon curd and

strawberry preserves, five tiers, color: light pink.

Pictures: taken at colt state park."

"Is there anything else I'm forgetting?" Delanie asked

herself as she dialed Kaydence's number to double

check that she had written down everything that

needed to happen, and she needed Kaydence's help to

put it into the exact order in which it would happen.

The Big Day

The angelic tone of *"Here comes the bride"* cascaded

from the piano as family and guests arose to welcome

the gorgeous bride. Sounds of amazement travelled

through the church as Delanie gracefully marched

down the aisle holding a perfectly crafted all white rose

bouquet with her pretty brown eyes peering through

the sheer cathedral veil directly at Tyson. He stood

with his hands folded in front of him as a wild smile spread across his face exposing his round planted dimples on the outside of his chocolate brown cheeks. Delanie felt like she was floating on air and everyone in the room had disappeared except her and Tyson. They kept their eyes glued to each other smiling endlessly throughout the entire ceremony. Delanie could hear the voice of Reverend Yasmin, cheers and laughter of friends and family members, but her body was in a state of trance. The reciting of the vows, exchanging of the rings, and the preaching all happened with Delanie staring deeply into Tyson's eyes. She was there, she was present. She spoke words and meant it but the moment was totally surreal. It was almost like an out of body experience when suddenly, the touch of Tyson's lips pressed against hers, broke off the trance. "Ladies and gentlemen, I now present to you Mr. and Mrs. Tyson Bailey!" The crowd cheered and for the first time Delanie saw clearly all the faces of her friends and loved ones clapping and cheering for her and Tyson. She smiled brightly as Tyson swept her off her feet out of the church into the limo. The rest of the bridal party joined them into the limo and they drove off to the park to take pictures before heading to the reception hall.

Lover Things

"*Mrs. Bailey,*" Tyson whispered softly into Delanie ears as she lay comfortably on the king sized bed in the presidential suite of the hotel downtown. "Yes Mr. Bailey," Delanie replied with a chuckle. "We did it," Tyson said as he placed wet kisses on her neck. Her white lace panties moistened from the touch of Tyson hands. "Oooh Mr. Bailey you're getting me really excited."

"Aaaahhh," she moaned with Tyson's strong muscular body pressed firmly against hers. "Yeah that is the plan. Come over here." He pulled her even closer to him and gripped her with his hands. "Wow I can't believe it," Delanie spoke as Tyson kissed on her collar bone. "Shhh there won't be much talking going on here young lady. I want you to lay down, close your eyes and just relax". Tyson's kisses descended from her collar bone, to between her breast down to her navel and then her inner thighs." Delanie felt like electrical beams had invaded her body. A fast rush of tingling sensation travelled through every part of her body causing her to jerk as Tyson continued to kiss and massage between her thighs. He rubbed them ever so softly. Delanie could feel her wetness slowly escaping her center making its way down her thighs. "Oh baby I want you," Delanie moaned with pleasure. "Not yet baby. I want to taste every bit of you." Tyson removed his hands from between her thighs grabbed her face and passionately kissed her lips. He stroked her hair as they tongue kissed. Her body shivered as he cupped her breasts and placed them in his mouth one at a time. "Oh my goodness," she screamed. "I want you so bad baby! Please let me have you," Delanie begged.

Tyson smiled as he released her breast from his mouth. "Your wish is my command, open up," he said as he separated her thighs. "Oh not yet baby. I too want to return the favor. Lay down," she said seductively. Tyson happily obliged. Delanie held his hard manhood with both hands. She licked the clear juices flowing from it and then placed it straight into her mouth. "Oooh Yes! Just like that baby," Tyson moaned. Delanie sucked and stroked it. "Oh that feels so good baby," Tyson's eyes rolled back. Pulling him out of her mouth she smiled and said, "I want to go on top." Tyson's manhood remained shooting straight up in the air as Delanie climbed on top. "This is how I like it," Delanie said as she slowly directed it into her center.

Chapter
-Thirteen-

Open Heart

"I'm coming!" Delanie yelled to Kaydence who was ringing the doorbell nonstop. *If she don't stop ringing that damn bell like that I swear—* Delanie thought to herself as she quickly tied on her robe and speed walked to the door to let Kaydence in. "It's about time you open this damn door it's freezing out here," Kaydence said as she slowly pushed passed Delanie and let herself into the house. "By the way marriage is certainly working for you, you're looking good girl. Although I see you're not wearing much of anything these days," Kaydence teased, took off her gloves and placed them in her jacket pocket. "Oh please child, I was trying to clean up real quick before you got here. Plus I didn't see any need to get all fancy. It's just you," Delanie teased back and took Kaydence's jacket from her. She put the jacket in the coat closet and they walked into the living room. "This place really looks nice Dee. I love your decor!" Kaydence said, admiring the inside of their home. "Thanks Kay. You should have seen it before I moved in here. It was a complete man cave." Delanie put the plate of crackers and cheese in front of Kaydence. "Do you want white or red wine?" Delanie asked showing Kaydence the bottles. "I'll do white please. I can see you certainly added some feminine touch. It looks really great," Kaydence complimented again as she took a sip of wine from her glass. "I'm so glad you came over Kay," Delanie said sitting down next to Kaydence. "Oh the pictures are ready, the photographer emailed them to us. She wants us to take a look at them and add any final comments or concerns before she puts them on a CD and flash drive for us to have." Delanie opened up her laptop, logged into her account and pulled up the pictures." Kaydence gasped at almost every photo. "These are beautiful Dee! I can't believe it! Look at you guys. You looked so stunning Dee!" Kaydence said smiling at the pictures as Delanie clicked through each one. "I know it's almost surreal. I mean I am married. Me married? And to an amazing guy at that! I never really dreamed that this could happen Kay." Delanie closed the laptop and stared at Kaydence in the eyes. "Every day I'm learning how to open my heart to this man. Some days are easier than others. Some days whether I want to or not thoughts creep into my mind," her voice began to crack up. "Dee you know you can't—" Kaydence interrupted. "I know Kay, trust me I know and I don't try to. Sometimes it's just hard not too you know. The truth is I am happy Kay. Like really happy. This man makes me laugh, he's caring and most of all he loves me so much! He is so kind to me. I'm so happy it hurts." Delanie's eyes welled up with tears. "Aww I am so happy for you. Tyson is a great guy and the two of you deserve each other." Kaydence smiled at her. "Now let's get more wine and continue to look at these pictures. I want to see how beautiful I looked," Delanie chuckled. She was glad that she and Kaydence got the chance to hang out and have some girl time. She opened up the laptop and they continued to look at the pictures. They reminisced and shared laughter about all the shenanigans that went down during the preparation for the wedding.

Chocolate Arms

"You fucking bitch you think it's funny how you got me waiting for you outside while you smile in another niggas face. You think I'm stupid!" Delanie fought for air as Ernest squeezed her neck with both arms. *"Please...I...can't...breathe..."* Delanie begged him, barely getting the words out from his grip. She struggled for air as Ernest strangled her. *"I should smack the shit out of you. That's how you like it. You piece of slut. You make me sick!"* Kicking and fussing Delanie fought to release herself from his stronghold. *"Ooooh noooo!!!"* she screamed jumping up and panting in a cold sweat.

Tyson held on to her firmly but gently. "It's okay babe. It's okay. It was just a bad dream. I'm here with you. You're safe," Tyson said as he planted soft kisses on her forehead. He felt her tears drip down on his arms. Tyson slowly wiped her face with his hands. "It's okay baby. Don't cry," he switched on the lamp. "Let me get you some water. You're sweating." He quickly went into the kitchen and brought back a tall glass of cold water. "Here drink some," Tyson said, handing her the water. Her hands trembled as she tried to take the glass out of Tyson's hand. "I got it." Tyson sat up beside her and fed her sips of water. Then he laid her head on his chest and he wrapped his arms around her. Delanie breathe slowly into his chocolate arms. She found so much solace in those arms. Delanie wondered how it was possible that she could lay comfortably in a set of chocolate arms which put her mind to ease and brought her so much joy, yet she was consistently struggling to erase the visions of those other pair of arms that brought her agony, arms

that nearly choked the breath out of her. She let out a

loud sigh and slowly began to close her eyes again.

Thankful to be lying safely in the arms of her husband

and not struggling to breathe under the arms of

Ernest.

Aroma

Tyson was really bothered by Delanie's nightmare. He

had asked her several times what was it that

frightened her but something in her eyes told him that

she was not quite ready to let him know what it was.

He did not want to pry. Tyson had assured Delanie

time and time again that there was nothing he

wouldn't do for her. As much as he wanted to know

what was bothering his wife, interrupting her sleep,

and keeping her screaming at night, he also did not

want to pressure her. He could tell that whatever it

was, it was beyond just a nightmare. The aromas of

Delanie's cooking always put a smile on his face. He could tell that she was whipping up something extremely delicious. Delanie was busy stirring the pot as Tyson tip toed and stood behind her. He gently placed his arms around her waist. Delanie jumped a little. "You startled me babe," she said turning around to face him. "My bad I didn't mean to scare you babe. What are you making?" Tyson asked. Delanie quickly placed the lid over the pot. "Uh-uh it's a surprise, I saw this recipe online and I thought why not try it? I hope you like it," Delanie lowered the stove, took Tyson by the hand a lead him to the dining room table. "Hey why are you trying to kick me out of the kitchen? Please just let me see it babe. I might not like it if I don't know what it is," Tyson teased.

"You'll like it. You like everything I make," Delanie teased back. She was nervous to tell Tyson about her past. She did not want his view of her to change once he knew the truth about her past. She still couldn't even believe how it was that she subjected herself to such abuse. Delanie knew Tyson truly loved her and he wouldn't do anything to cause her any harm or pain, so now was the time that he knew the truth behind her nightmares.

Chapter

-Fourteen-

An Hour

"Yeah that's right ride this dick hoe. Yeah go ahead take it all in. Bitch don't you choke on this dick," groaning and moaning penetrated through the walls as Ernest covered his ears with his pillow. He tossed and turned wishing he could make the whole thing disappear. His brother Ralph was old enough to leave the house and go over to his friends' house. Young Ernest was stuck inside keeping watch and tracking the time. He hated doing it but he had to do it to avoid a whooping. Pounding on the door Ernest screamed "It's been an hour! An hour mama!" Just then the man walked out of the room with his pants unzipped. "Same time next week," he said, as he zipped up his pants. 'What's up lil' nigga?' he brushed past Ernest nearly knocking him to the ground. Ernest snuck his head in the bedroom door to peak and see if his mother was okay. "I'm getting dress! Shut the damn door before I slap the shit outta you!" Ernest quickly shut the door

without any hesitation. "Are you okay mama?" There were times Ernest actually heard his mother crying. Sometimes she walked out of the room with bruises all over her body. One time one of the men slapped her so hard she passed out. The man came running out the door. When Ernest entered in the room he saw his mother's lifeless body lying on the bed. Thankfully, Ralph had walked into the house just in time. Ernest went crying to Ralph. "Something happened to mama. She's not moving!" "I don't fucking care," Ralph said nonchalantly. "Ralph please you gotta see. Mama's not moving!" Ernest pleaded. Finally Ralph called 911 and the ambulance came and took her. Ernest did not want that to happen again so as much as he hated keeping track of the time he did it anyway. His mother walked into the living room where Ernest was sitting playing his X-box. He found solace in his war game. It served as a distraction for all the chaos that was happening in his house. Ernest did not quite understand what exactly went on in the room but he knew one thing for sure, his mother always walked funny whenever she came out. She always looked like she was in pain. Ernest also couldn't understand why his brother Ralph was always mad at their mother. Ralph would cuss her out and argue with her. "Are you all right mama?" Ernest paused his game and looked at his mother. "Boy pass me my lighter don't be worried about if I'm all right or not. All you need to do is make sure you don't let an hour pass by without knocking on that door. You hear?" "Yes mama," Ernest answered. He was nine years old and his brother Ralph was thirteen when their mother passed away from a drug overdose. The state took them and he hadn't seen his brother since. Ernest regretted many things in his life but meeting Delanie wasn't one of them. Delanie had seen a side of him that he didn't even know he had. When did he develop so much anger? Years had gone by since he left Rhode Island, but not a moment had passed without him thinking about Delanie. If only he could get an hour of her time.

The Other Side of Love

"I love you Delanie I really do," Ernest said as he held her in his arms. He pressed down the swell on her lips with a cold wet towel. "I promise I'll change. I'll stop smoking. I'll get some help Delanie, I promise. Please don't leave me." Delanie lay helplessly on the bed. Ernest ranted on about how much he loved her and how he'd do anything to keep her in his life. "Please Dee don't tell anyone about this. You know I don't be meaning to hurt you. I got to control my anger I know. Trust me I'm going to change. You are the best thing that ever happened to me." Ernest looked over at Delanie who was slowly drifting to sleep. Shaking her, he said "You hear me Dee? You're the best thing that ever happened to me. I have nobody. You're the only person I have," Delanie did not respond. "Answer me

Dee! Say you're not going to leave me!" He shook her harder. "I'm not going to leave you," Delanie said in a whisper. "You have to promise Dee. Promise that we're going to be together when I get back from New York. I'm only going to be gone for the semester. I have to take this internship Dee but you have to promise that we'll still be together even when I'm gone. Please Dee I'm begging you." Delanie sat up on the bed and saw the tears filled up in his eyes. She wondered why the hell he was crying when she was the one with the busted up lip. "I promise we'll still be together Ernest. I love you too." Ernest smiled at the memory of the last face to face conversation he had with Delanie before leaving for New York. He spoke with Delanie over the phone when he first moved. She made him believe that they were still together. She was the one who encouraged him to stay in New York and take the job offer. He believed in their love but now Ernest could see why Delanie cut out all contact with him. Sometimes we can run away from our past but we can't hide from it. The past has its way of catching up with you.

365 Days

The alarm went off and Delanie searched for her cell phone under the pillow case. She pressed snooze and was about to shut her eyes again when she began smelling the sweet aroma of hazelnut coffee foaming through the cracks of her bedroom door. Delanie got out of bed and slipped on her silky white robe with pink fluffy house slippers. It was 5:30am and she was surprised that Tyson was up this early on a Saturday morning, and making coffee at that.

Reluctantly dragging her feet, she strolled into the kitchen where her eyes met this 6 foot, chocolate, well-cut biceps, giant, standing shirtless in the middle of their kitchen.

His pearl white smile cut sleep residues right out of her eyes as he gently embraced her, placing long wet kisses on her lips.

"Good morning, Sunshine. I made your coffee," he said. Smiling but still a little puzzled, she took a sip of the rich, creamy better than Starbucks coffee.

"Hmmm...Good morning indeed," she said shocked as she thought about why he was up early.

"Baby, what are you doing up at this time?"

As a mechanical engineer, Tyson worked Monday through Friday and had the weekend off. Still smiling in between taking sips of her coffee, she stared at him amazed by how surprisingly sweet he could be at times. This was a nice surprise, especially knowing how much he loved to sleep in on Saturdays.

Delanie imagined how time flies, a year ago she and Tyson exchanged vows at a very small intimate ceremony at their local church. 365 days later she was still on cloud nine.

"Well, I know how much you don't totally look forward to working on Saturdays," Tyson said.

"Hmm...continue," Delanie replied.

"So I thought it would be kind of me to make you a cup of coffee to help cheer you up. Plus I have something else I would like to give you, and I thought this would be a good way to wake you up," he replied.

Delanie gave him the "I know what this is about look," but before she could utter the words, he picked her up and escorted her back to their bedroom with the scent of coffee trailing behind them.

"So this was your plan? Caffeine me up and take advantage of me?" she jokingly said. They both laughed as she braced her mind for the heavenly encounter that was about to take place between them. It was mornings like these that made her late for work, thankfully it was Saturday and she only had to be at work for three hours for a professional training. Tyson began to kiss her on the neck. Delanie lied on top of Tyson with her head placed on his chest listening to his heart beat. Delanie loved the way Tyson embraced her every time she laid on top of him. She truly wanted to engage in this heavenly encounter but she knew there was no such thing as a "quickie" when it came to her husband. "Babe I would love to do this but I truly don't have time." Ignoring her Tyson continued to slowly rub his hands up and down her back. He touched and squeezed her butt cheeks. Delanie squealed, laughed, and jumped up from on top of him, pulling the covers with her.

"Why are you doing all that? You know I love to see you naked," Tyson teased. Tying the sheets tightly around her breast Delanie turned to him. "Yes but I really have to get my naked butt in the shower. It's cold. We need to turn up the heat and by 'we' I mean you." Tyson grabbed his boxer off the floor and put it on. "Of course you do." He pecked her on the cheek then walked over and turned up the heat. "What are your plans for today babe?" Delanie called out from the shower. She always had to find strategic ways to navigate her way from under Tyson's sweet embrace, otherwise she would spend the rest of her days and hours just being up under him and nothing would get done. Delanie loved cuddling up with her husband.

"I'm linking up with Charles at noon," he hollered.

"Why? Do you want us to continue this love-making session that we didn't get to after you leave work?" Tyson teased. "Baby you might actually have a problem. You love sex way too much," Delanie teased back. "Well we are technically still newlyweds and this is still our honeymoon phase," Tyson replied. "You are milking this newlywed phase a little. It's been a year babe. But seriously I would like to try this new Jamaican restaurant after I get back from the nail salon with Kaydence."

"Sure we can do that. Anything for you sexy," Tyson said sliding back the shower curtain. "Boy bye. Close this curtain," Delanie said laughing.

Spa day

"Girl I am long overdue for a manicure," Delanie said, staring at how the acrylic was beginning to slowly creep off her finger nails exposing a gap between her nail bed and showing off her real nails. "Me too hunnii, I'm so ashamed to show them I teach with my hands ball up into a fist like ready to fight these kids." Delanie burst out laughing. "Girl you are such a clown. I can't with you." They walked over to the massage chair and sat down. "It's packed in here, good thing we made reservations or we wouldn't have been able to wait," Delanie said turning on the button on the massage chair. "I know," Kaydence agreed. "Kay listen I'm been having a real strange feeling lately I don't know what it is." Kaydence digs into her purse as Delanie is talking. "I have been light headed and I don't have much of an appetite. I thought about going to the doctor but then I said maybe it's just stress from work and you know with..." Kaydence pulls a box of brand-new pregnancy tests out of her purse and handed it to Delanie. "Here take this," she said placing it on Delanie's lap. "Why the hell do you have a pregnancy test in your purse?" Delanie asked in disbelief. "Girl we have not had the time to talk much but I had a little scare a few days ago and decided to buy some just to be safe," Kaydence said. "A scare with who?" Delanie felt a little guilty for not talking with Kaydence more often. She did not want them to go long without talking like they did in college. Delanie knows that if you let too much time pass by, it has a way of wiping away relationship.

"Girl no one important I'll tell you about it when we get in the car." Kaydence sure did have a way of keeping Delanie on her toes. Delanie and Tyson were not really trying, they were simply enjoying the process, but she guessed it wouldn't hurt to take a test. Delanie took the test and put it in her purse. "I'll let you know the results once I take it," Delanie said smiling. "Please do, I can't wait to be an aunty to spoil my little niece or nephew," Kaydence added. "I bet you can't," Delanie said, "And I can't wait to hear about this mystery guy of yours." "Girl please it's more of a recycle, I want to keep my numbers low ya know?" Kaydence laughed. "Oh no the hell you didn't!" Delanie already knew who it was. "Please spare me the details," she said teasing. After the nail salon Delanie dropped off Kaydence. Delanie pulled into the drive way still laughing at the thought of Kaydence and home dude hooking up again.

"I got to remind Tyson to put some salt on the driveway. It's really slippery," she said aloud. She took out her cell phone and didn't have one missed called from Tyson. *He must be having fun with Charles,* she thought. Delanie took out her cell phone and was about to call Tyson when his call started to come in. She smiled at how frequently this usually happens.

"Hello Babe. Having fun with Charles?"

"Hmmm yeah— we were but I'm at the hospital," Tyson

said nonchalantly trying not to alarm her. "I'll be right there," Delanie said. "Okay sweetheart take your time. No rush. Charles' here with me," Tyson said. He was growing tired of battling this but he had to remain strong especially for Delanie. Hanging up the phone Delanie sighed heavily. She wondered how long Tyson would be in the hospital this time. "Perhaps I should pack an overnight bag just in case," she thought as she headed into the house. She quickly packed an overnight bag. If Tyson had to sleep at the hospital then that meant she'd have to sleep at the hospital. She had gotten too used to sleeping with him night after night and there was no way that she'd be spending the night alone. Delanie took the pregnancy test out of her purse and stared at it. "Should I pee on it now or later?" she asked herself. "Later," she decided and put it back into her purse. The minute she entered into the hospital Delanie began to feel nauseous. She went into the bathroom immediately after entering into Tyson's room and puked into the toilet. "Hey what's going on I'm supposed to be the sick one remember?" Tyson called out to her. Oh how she wished that statement wasn't true. "I hate hospitals babe. It just makes me so nauseous. I can't believe I actually puked though," Delanie said, turning on the faucet as she washed her hands and face. She stepped out of the bathroom. "How are you babe?" The answer was obvious. She greeted Charles who was sitting in the chair on the side of Tyson. Charles really is a good friend. He's more like Tyson's brother. Delanie thought as she hugged Charles. "So what did the doctor say, are we going to be here long? I mean you know, is it going to be weeks, days, because I already packed an overnight bag but I can also go back home and pack more stuff." Overnight visits to the hospital had become part of Delanie's life now. "No I don't think so. I should be out of here in a few hours. Come here," Tyson said patting the bed for Delanie to sit next to him. "Thank goodness," Delanie thought, as she sat

next to Tyson.

Chapter

-Fifteen-

Darkness Falls

Some say there is no place like home but sometimes home comes with a lot of darkness and pain regardless, like the saying goes home is home and there's truly no place like home. This eerie feeling Ernest felt were feelings of his past. The flight had delayed and he didn't land until after midnight. Ernest always hated the midnight hour. It was the darkest time of his life. Midnight brought flocks of men flowing in and out of his house when he was a child. He wished he would have been strong enough to tell Delanie about his childhood. They never really discussed it. He wanted to tell her about what it was like for him growing up with a mother who prostituted for a living and used hard core drugs, but all he told her was that his mother passed when he was very young. Delanie was a breath of fresh air for him. She was nothing like his mother when he first met her.

Delanie always wanted to spend time with him. Ernest had never felt so loved than he did when he and Delanie's relationship first began. Somehow it seemed that Delanie was beginning to grow tired of their time together. She expressed to him over and over again how she needed to spend some time with her friends. Ernest did not understand why she no longer wanted to be around him anymore when it was all that he wanted to do. Feelings of abandonment and neglect begin to resurface. He did not choose the brightest way to deal with those feelings. He understood that now. As he sat at the airport thoughts of those dark moments from his childhood visited his mind. A cluster of sounds from the voices of strange men saying all sorts of degrading and nasty things to his mother began to ring in his ears. Ernest pulled out his cell phone, requested for a cab, plugged in his ear phones and played his music selection. The song that came on reminded him of Delanie. It was one of their favorite songs. He remembered how they used to ride around campus at night listening to slow jams. Ernest thought about how much he was in love with Delanie. He was infatuated and obsessed with her. Waiting for her outside of her classes was his way of protecting and guarding her. He did not like when different guys would cut in while they were dancing at a party. It would really upset him how freely Delanie would go along with it. It reminded him of how different men used his mother. He just could not stand to see that happen to yet another woman he loved. Ernest blamed Delanie for allowing those guys to dance up all on her and especially for doing it in front of him. The mere thought of Delanie being with any other guy sent anger through the core of him. He felt bad for Delanie. He wanted to stop. He wanted to love her differently but he just didn't know how. Ernest pulled his suitcases into the trunk of the taxi cab, got in and sat down. "Where to?" the driver asked. "Providence," Ernest responded as thoughts of Delanie continued to float in his mind.

V-Day

It wasn't even a real holiday with all the hype that went into it. There's going to be overpriced food at all restaurants, which will be filled to capacity, yet there will still be people standing out in the cold just to get a bite to eat and express their love to someone, not to mention long lines at every store and venders selling flowers, cards, and candy at each street corner. People should at least get the day off to deal with all the chaos of Valentine's Day, but unfortunately that was not the case.

Everybody had to work and yet be expected to go home and then head to some restaurant to express their love. Delanie did not need one special day to tell Tyson how much she loved him and vice versa, however it was Valentine's Day and as much as she disliked V-Day she could not let it pass them by without some form of celebrating. It was brick cold out and the thought of standing in line for more than fifteen minutes just to pick up an item or two was overwhelming.

However Delanie wanted to do something special for her hubby.

She rushed to the store and bought three bouquets of red and pink roses. Thankfully the line wasn't as long as she expected. She had a million and one cute ideas of what she wanted to do but she needed to hurry up before Tyson got home. She looked at the clock in the kitchen as she placed her bags down. She had approximately forty-five minutes to prep the house, shower, and slip into something sexy before Tyson walked through those doors. She had a new set of sexy panties which Tyson had yet to lay eyes on. *I think I will wear that one,* she thought to herself. Now all she needed was a matching bra to go with it. He has seen her entire bra collection. "No bra," she said aloud.

Delanie turned on the shower got in and quickly

freshened up, she then headed into the bedroom

pulled one of Tyson's long sleeve shirts out of the

closet and a pair of her favorite nude heals. *This will*

do the trick, she smiled as she pulled the black and red

lace panties from her drawer. That's the outfit for the

night she thought. Delanie walked back into the

kitchen, took the bouquet of flowers and peeled off the

rose petals. She sprinkled the rose petals on the floor,

creating a trail leading to their bedroom. Delanie

turned on the smart TV and played her romance

playlist on her YouTube channel. Songs of love-making

echoed through the house. She went into the

bathroom and placed red and white tea light candles

around the bathtub. Filling the tub with warm water,

she poured in the bubble bath. She then sprinkled

some rose petals onto the foam of the bubble bath.

Just then she heard keys rattling in the door. "Oh

shoot I'm not done yet." She still needed to slip into

her outfit. "Babe don't come in yet!" She yelled, but Tyson had already entered and seen the trail of rose petals leading to their bedroom. "No baby you have to go back out please," Delanie begged laughing as she poked her head out of the bathroom. "Okay," Tyson replied smiling. He loved how thoughtful and romantic Delanie could be. Obediently he stepped back out and waited for her signal to come back in. She quickly put on her outfit sprayed on some perfume, hid behind the front door and called to Tyson. "You can come in now". Tyson walked in and handed Delanie a dozen red roses and a tiffany box. "You look great babe," he said kissing her. Tyson was already turned on. "Thanks babe," Delanie blushed as she took the flowers and gift from Tyson. "I thought we agreed that we won't be exchanging gifts?" she asked surprised. Tyson knew better though. "This is just a small token of my appreciation for you babe," he said kissing her. She opened it and saw the beautiful diamond bracelet. "Oh babe I love it!" Delanie was glad Tyson did not listen to her about the no gift exchanging thing but now she felt bad for not buying him anything.

"Wait right here. I'll be right back," Delanie strutted into the bed room and grabbed the box she had wrapped earlier. "Go ahead open your gift," she said handing him the box. He peeled the wrapper off and stared at the IPad mini box which he had gotten her for Christmas. "Babe you re-gifted me?" He said laughing. "No, No, No, open it," Delanie said. He opened the box and stared at the pregnancy test stick displaying the word "PREGNANT". He was stunned. "Are you serious babe? Is it true?" He asked with excitement. "Well, we'll know for sure tomorrow after my appointment with my OBG-YN but for now…yes it looks like it," Delanie said touching her stomach. Tyson picked her up and planted kisses all over her belly. "I love you! I love you!" He screamed and spun her around. "Oh my God stop babe I'm going to throw up," Delanie said laughing. "You can puke all over me," Tyson said as he continued to spin her. "Wait does that mean we can't bump and grind tonight because—you know—you have a little person growing inside of you, cause I got to give it to you my shirt has never looked as good on me as it does on you. You got a brother hot and bothered," Tyson teased. "Well, it was all that bumping and grinding that got us here so I don't see why we can't do more," Delanie said seductively as she held his hand and led him into the bedroom.

Lime not Lemon

Morning sickness is a lie. For Delanie it was all day and all night sickness. She couldn't seem to keep anything down. One of her African clients told her to lick a lime before eating and it would help to keep the food down. Delanie recalled their conversation that day and how hilarious it was. She said "Honey you know how Americans have the saying when life throws you lemons make lemonade?" Before Delanie could respond she continued, "Well life so tough for me in Africa it didn't even give me lemons all I had were limes. I tried to make lime-aid but the juice was way too sour. I threw that lime right back. I'm a lime backer. You know what sometimes when life gives you crap you have to throw that crap right back. That's my saying." Delanie burst out laughing. "Oh yeah lime is not all that bad. It'll help you keep your food down and help with the throwing up." Delanie had to admit that was one of her favorite clients. She was way too funny and always trying to talk "American" as she put it in her beautiful African accent. Delanie wondered if the throwing up would continue throughout her entire pregnancy. "Why are you buying all these limes?" Kaydence asked as they stood in the produce isle of the grocery store. "One of my clients said it would help me keep the food down. I figured why not try it,"

Delanie replied. "Oh I see. How are you feeling besides the whole throwing up thing?" Kaydence asked. "Girl that's just it, other than that I am doing just fine." "And how is Tyson doing? I know he's super excited," Kaydence said as they walked through the isle. "Girl he doesn't want me to lift a finger. I have to keep reminding him that I'm pregnant not handicap. He's so sweet though Kay. I have not done one bit of house work since I broke the news to him and the doctor confirmed it," Delanie said smiling. "It's great but it's driving me crazy. He doesn't want me to do anything, I mean anything! Shoot he doesn't even want me working." "Oh lord, he's really going overboard isn't he?" Kaydence asked. "You have no idea. 'Overboard' is an understatement," Delanie said pushing the cart to the self-check out. "I can't believe you are three months already. You're barely showing and your skin is flawless. I think it's a boy," Kaydence said. "Oh my goodness that's funny because Tyson swears that I'm having a boy also. I don't want to know the sex though." "Wait, what?" Kaydence asked surprised. "What about Tyson?" "Oh he definitely wants to know. He just got to keep it a secret. My OBG-YN said we will be able to tell with certainty around 18-21 weeks," Delanie said. "Girl what the hell does that mean? I hate when mothers talk in terms of weeks just tell me in months so I can start shopping for my nephew," Kaydence said teasing. "Oh my bad four to five months," Delanie said as she scanned the groceries. "Oh that's pretty soon then," Kaydence added. "It is, and honestly I don't care if it's a boy or girl. I just want a healthy baby Kay. You know what I mean?" Kaydence knew exactly what she meant.

Chapter

-Sixteen-

Running

Sweat dripped down from his face into his eyes as he ran. Ernest was growing tired and needed a cup of water to cool down. His stomach began to growl signaling that he needed to eat something as well. He was starting to feel light headed from all that running. It was time for him to take a break. He opened the restaurant door and stood in line. There was a woman in front of him who could not decide what it is she wanted. The cashier was very patient with her. For some reason she was not in any hurry to rush the lady or take the next customer order. Ernest thought about turning around to leave but just when he was about to do so the woman started placing her order. *Thank goodness*, he thought to himself. A sound of familiarity struck him as he listened to the sound of the woman's voice. In the middle of placing in her order she pulled out her cell phone and said to the cashier "I'm sorry but I really have to respond to this text quickly. You can take the next person." The woman stepped aside with her face glued down to the screen of the phone. The cashier turned to Ernest and said "How can I help you sir?" Ernest waved never mind and walked out. He could not believe what his eyes just saw. A part of him wanted to say something but he simply could not find the words. "I should go back in there," he said to himself as the woman opened the restaurant door walking out with her food in hand. "It's too late," Ernest thought. He had gotten a clear view of her but she did not see him. He walked back in the restaurant and overheard the cashier saying to her co-worker, "It is so cute how she comes in here every day takes long to decide what she wants but always ends up ordering the same thing." The co-worker smiled at the cashier and added, "Yeah she's real cute and friendly. I like how she always greets us by our name. For as long as I've been working here she is the only customer who does that," Ernest knew instantly what he had to do.

No more running.

Nightmare on Ernest's Street

Delanie held on tightly to the steering wheel. Fear gripped her as her body tensed up. She was usually careful to avoid this street, but with all the construction going on the road she typically went, the signs of detours had led her right to it. Delanie grew upset with herself for leaving the house. She could feel her memory box opening up as she sat in the bumper to bumper traffic waiting on cars to drive. The memories began to explode in her head like a volcano. *It was 2:42am they had just come from dancing at a local club downtown. Delanie was driving her hooptie when she heard a funny sound coming from the car. Ernest was too drunk to care and she was too pissed to say anything to him. How disrespectful of him, she thought. She could not wait to drop him off at home and head back to campus. He looked up at her with the* stench of alcohol fuming from his breath. "Don't think I didn't see you talking to that skinny nigga. I bet you're fucking him." Delanie simply rolled her eyes without saying a word. "Answer me bitch! Are you fucking him?!" Before Delanie could answer he abruptly changed the gear and put the car in park. "What are doing?!" she screamed in a panic. "Bitch don't be driving when I'm trying to talk to you!" He screamed back at her. "You're drunk Ernest and I need to get back on campus," Delanie said softly. "I ain't drunk," he said as he tried pulling her close to him. "Smell my breath." He opened his mouth wide. "Ernest please you're drunk," she pleaded but within seconds a slab of cold saliva hit her in the face like a ton of bricks. She felt lower than dirt as she wiped away a mixture of his spit and tears off her face. "Why did you do that Ernest? Why did you spit in my face?' she asked crying. Her skin grew increasingly hot and every muscle in her body stiffened. She wanted so badly to hit him but she *remembered from time past that her strength did not*

measure up to his. Ernest sat slugged back with a

smirk on his face knowing that there was nothing she

do could about it. Delanie turned the key in the ignition

but the car would not start. "What the hell are you

doing? Drive you stupid bitch!" He yelled at her. "I can't

the car won't start," she said. Delanie wondered why

he hated her so much. Every little thing she did seemed

to upset him. Ernest sat up, opened the car door and got

out. "Where are you going?" Delanie asked hoping that

he was going to take a look at the car to find out what

was wrong with it. "Home I'm only two blocks from

here," he responded as he walked down the pitch black

street. Delanie followed him. "Where do you think

you're going?" He stopped walking and turned around

to her. "With you," she said shaking with nervousness.

As much as she did not want to go with him she figured

she had no other choice. "No you're not, I got

roommates," Ernest said coldly. She could not believe

that after all those times he slept over in her dorm room with her he now had the audacity to tell her she could not spend the night at his house. She ignored him and continued to follow him. There was nothing else that she could really do at that moment. "Bitch I told you you're not fucking going with me!" Ernest said pushing her with all his force to the ground. Delanie sat on the cold cement pavement watching him walk away without a care in the world. After what seemed like an eternity she eventually picked herself back up turned in the opposite direction and walked back over to her car. She was way too ashamed to call anyone. That side of town was notorious for crimes. She entered in the car, locked the doors and laid in the back seat where she fell asleep until the next day. Some believe in chances and others believe in miracles, but for Delanie, it was nothing short of a miracle that she survived. It was certain that a divine force guarded her that night. Her stomach began to jump, she felt the kicking of her baby and the reminder of the love growing inside her closed that memory box. Delanie trembled at the thought of the nightmare she experienced on that street, when the blinking light from a car signaling her to go brought her mind back to complete focus. She drove on to get her favorite treat and satisfied the cravings of her little love bug. Delanie kept one hand on her belly and the other on the steering wheel as she drove, she needed to continue to feel the love inside of her. She had really taken some bold steps to free her mind from those awful memories. One of the best steps she took was marrying Tyson. The image of Tyson's face put the brightest smile on her face.

The Messenger

The struggle is real, Kaydence thought as she shampooed her hair. She did not have money to go to a salon but her natural hair had not been cooperating at all this week. She stopped by her local beauty shop and bought three packs of braiding hair to do her own box braids. After hours of tutorials on the internet she could only hope that she had grasped the concept of braiding her own hair. *There's only one way to find out,* she thought. Kaydence shampooed and conditioned her hair in the bathroom. Then she plugged in the blow dryer, stood in front of the mirror and blow dried her hair. When she was finished she went to grab the braiding hair out of the living room and she noticed four missed calls from an unfamiliar number. She was going to call the number back but she noticed her voicemail indicator was also flashing. Should I listen to the voicemail or call back, she questioned herself. She decided to call the number back. "Hello? Is this Kaydence?" The voice on the other side sounded frantic and nervous. "Yes this is Kaydence, who is this?" Kaydence could tell it was an older woman on the other end but she had no idea who she was. "Great Kaydence listen to me I need you to please—"

The voice on the phone continued as Kaydence listened attentively. She felt chills moving through her body. After hanging up the call she did not know what to do. "Kaydence," The woman called her name. "Kaydence did you hear everything I just said?" Kaydence heard everything but she was just frozen. "Yes ma'am I did but—" the woman interrupted her before she could continue. "I can't really say anymore please Kaydence just do what I've instructed you to do. It'll be a great help to us. Do you think you can do that?" Stuttering to get her words out she responded, "I...I... sure...I can do...it."

"Thank you Kaydence you're a great help to this family." The woman ended the call.

Kaydence's jaw dropped. This is too much, she could not carry this message alone. There was no way possible. No she was going to need back up, some assistance, some support. How could she deliver this type of message? She picked up her cell phone and texted Delanie. Kaydence was now sweating profusely, she was trying to make sense of what it was that was happening, but she just could not process it all. Hopefully this would not alarm Delanie but she needed Reverend Yasmin's number. Kaydence checked her phone and saw that Delanie sent the number with no question. She quickly dialed Reverend Yasmin's number and introduced herself. They spoke for almost two hours. Kaydence cried over the phone and reverend Yasmin assured her that everything would be okay. All they could do now is pray. "If prayer really works then it needs to work now, we need a miracle this is the worst possible timing," Kaydence said to Reverend Yasmin. "I understand your frustration honey but the Almighty always has a plan. He is the author and finisher of our life. Let me get dressed so I can come and meet you. We can go over together," Reverend Yasmin said. "Thank you so much Reverend, may God continues to bless you, because I don't think

I will be able to do this alone," Kaydence said as they

ended the call.

Chapter

-Seventeen-

Small Pleasures

Delanie did not think that this craving would continue

all the way into her third trimester. There were nights

where she had to wake Tyson up so he could make a

run to get her must have sundae. Tyson was truly an

amazing man. Delanie thought of the time she wanted

a hot fudge sundae. He went to the grocery store

bought vanilla ice-cream and hot fudge. He prepared

the sundae for her and carried it into the bedroom.

She took a spoon full of it and started crying. "Babe

what's the matter?" He asked confused. "I don't want

this. I want a hot fudge sundae from McDonald's," she

whined. Even Delanie could not understand why the

sundae had to come from McDonald's. Any other hot

fudge sundae just did not taste the same to her.

Delanie wanted to hurry up, get her sundae and go to

the hospital to her husband. Tyson had been in the

hospital for four days now. If it was not for her gigantic

belly and him insisting that she spend the night at

home, she would have been curled up right in that bed with him. Delanie smiled at the thought of all those times she and Tyson got freaky and did the nasty in the hospital bed. One time they almost got caught by the nurse. She missed her husband but he needed to be well enough to come home. Delanie had done some research on bone marrow transplant for sickle cell patients and hoped their child would be a match for Tyson. Of course there was a chance that the child could be a carrier of the disease and Delanie had been praying with all her might that the child would be a match. Watching Tyson suffer and having to be in and out of the hospital was heart breaking enough. She would not have been able to watch two people she loved go through the same thing, thankfully she would not have to. The only sure way to know if the child would be a match was for the doctors to run their tests and confirm after she gives birth. She pulled into the McDonald's parking lot and a sense of relief came over her. It is incredible how the small things in life can bring a person so much pleasure at times. Delanie had become a regular at that particular McDonald's. Practically every employee knew her as the pregnant lady who came in for the hot fudge sundae. She no longer needed to look at the cashiers' name tags. She knew each one by name and face. Delanie smiled when she saw the text from Kaydence. She sent Reverend Yasmin's number to her. Delanie knew that Kaydence had been going through some things lately but she did not want to tell Delanie exactly what it was. Delanie had tried encouraging Kaydence to visit their church but she had declined the offer on many occasions. *Well if anyone could convince Kaydence it sure would be Reverend Yasmin, she has such a way with people,* Delanie thought. Delanie had spoken highly of Reverend Yasmin to Kaydence numerous times. Perhaps Kaydence was ready to give church a try or at least consider it. After replying to the text she looked up at the cashier. "Hey you must be new," Delanie said. "Yes I just started today," the girl replied. "Well then in that case let me tell you what I want," Delanie placed her order. The coins fell out of her hands as she tried to take the sundae and pay the cashier at the same time. The man standing behind her picked it up. "Here you go Miss," Delanie turned around to get the money. She froze as she laid eyes on the man handing her the money. "Ernest?" She asked. Delanie dropped the sundae and instantly felt water sliding down her inner thighs. "Call the ambulance!" the new cashier screamed.

Man Up

Ernest had gotten tired of hiding himself from Delanie. Every day he visited that McDonald's, ordered something and waited for Delanie to come in. He knew her routine and every day he told himself that today would be the day he'll talk to her. Today will be the day he man up. He wanted her to know he was no longer that awful person she used to know. Now it was his chance to prove it. "No it's okay I will drive her. We know each other," Delanie heard Ernest say to the cashier. The strong cramp like pain travelled through her abdomen causing aches to her back. "I'm not going anywhere with you!" Delanie screamed in protest. "Delanie please I can drive you to the hospital faster than the ambulance can get here," Ernest pleaded. Delanie swung her pocketbook at him and he grabbed it. "Don't you dare touch me!" she hollered in more pain. The workers had already called the ambulance and within seconds sounds of sirens approached the building. Customers and employees gathered around as the EMT workers took Delanie on the stretcher. Ernest walked over to the ambulance, not wanting to give up easily. "I know this woman is it okay if I came along with her?" He asked the workers. "Hurry up, get in we don't have much time," one of the EMT workers said to him. "Don't you dare come anywhere near me," Delanie snared with so much hate in her voice. The EMT workers stared at each other with a confused stare. "Sir I'm sorry you'll have to get out. You're causing her a lot of distress." Ernest jumped down from the ambulance without hesitation. He desperately wanted to own up to all the horrible things he had done to her but he certainly did not want to cause her any more pain than she had or was in at this very moment. Delanie continued to cry in more pain as her contractions worsened. "Ma'am I'm afraid we're not going to be able to make it to the hospital. You are ten centimeters dilated," the worker told her. "NOOOO!!! I need to get to the hospital!" She screamed. "Ma'am I need you to trust me we will get you to the hospital but not right now. Right now you are having this baby. So on three I want you to push," the worker responded calmly. Delanie cried in more pain. "No it can't be! My husband he needs to be here!" Delanie tried to negotiate. "Ma'am listen to me, everything is going to be okay. This baby is coming. You have to push ma'am you can do it. Hold my hand and on the count of three..." the worker counted and on three Delanie gave the greatest push of her life and out came the precious cry of a tiny person. Workers and customers clapped and cheered as the ambulance drove off. With all the commotion going on Ernest did not realize that he was still holding on to Delanie's pocketbook until after the ambulance had driven off. He was not sure what to do as he stared at her pocketbook for a while, then got into his car and drove to the hospital.

Not Born Monsters

Ernest nervously drove to the hospital with Delanie's pocketbook on the passenger side. He stared at it in disbelief. All this time he planned on what he'd say to Delanie when he finally saw her. Never did he imagine the situation or circumstances would be like this.

Delanie was truly a God send in his life at the time they were together and he was nothing but the devil himself towards her. If only he could turn back the hands of time. He needed to do something good for Delanie even if it was just this one time. It was certain that he was the last person she needed or wanted to see at this moment in her life. Ernest couldn't say he blamed her either. He pulled up to the hospital parking lot, took a parking ticket, and parked his car. He sat with both his hands on the steering wheel. He thought about how much of a long fight it had been for him to get rid of the anger he carried in his heart for how his mother chose to live and end her life. The monster that had grown inside of him needed to be buried for good. He was not born with this monster. However he had cultivated it as a shield of protection from his then reality. No way was he going to allow this monster to live another day. In fact he needed to show Delanie and everyone else that he wasn't born a monster. Ernest reached into her pocketbook and pulled out her cellphone. Delanie needed to have someone she loved and cared for by her side and he definitely was not the one. "Call Kaydence," he spoke into the phone. "Calling Kaydence," the phone replied. He had been right, Kaydence and Delanie were thick as thieves, and even he could not come in between their friendship. Ernest knew that Delanie and Kaydence were as different as day and night. Kaydence was indeed a firecracker so he was not quite sure exactly what to expect when he saw her. Ernest did his best explaining the situation to Kaydence. Much to his surprised she was very calm over the phone. He paced back and forth in the lobby awaiting Kaydence's arrival.

Chapter

- Eighteen -

Welcome

Thirty minutes later Kaydence rushed through the doors of the hospital. A furious slap greeted Ernest across his face when she approached him. "Don't you dare think because you happened to *'show up'* in a moment like this that all is forgotten," she hurled at him and snatched Delanie's pocketbook out of his hands with a look of disgust featured on her face. "Kaydence...I'm sure..." Ernest began to stutter. "Don't say a word to me! This is not the time or the place," Kaydence interrupted, looking him up and down. "You can go. I'm here now," she ordered him. Kaydence stood with her arms crossed over her chest and waited for Ernest to walk out of the hospital. He turned and walked away without hesitation. Kaydence rolled her eyes as she walked towards the elevator. She pressed the "up" button arrow on the elevator and entered into it. Kaydence slowly opened Delanie's room door. "Hey hunnii...I'm here," she said with excitement as she walked over to Delanie. "Hey Kay thank God you're here," Delanie said as she adjusted her pillow with the baby in her arms. "TJ say hello to aunty Kaydence," Delanie said handing the baby to Kaydence. "Give me a second TJ, Aunty Kay needs to wash her hands," she hurried to the sink, quickly washed her hands and took TJ into her arms. "Oh my God Dee! He's beautiful!" Kaydence smiled from ear to ear while starring into the eyes of TJ. "Welcome baby boy," Kaydence said as she rocked him in her arms. She then took a seat in the chair next to Delanie's bed. "So how are you feeling?" Kaydence asked without taking her eyes off of TJ. Delanie sat up in the bed. "Kay I can't even bring myself to wrap my head around what happened. I mean when I turn around and saw him—" she sighed. "I smacked the heck out of him the minute I laid eyes on him don't you worry about any of that now Dee I made sure he left," Kaydence assured her. "The important thing is you and the baby are fine,"

Kaydence added. "Yes thank God for that. I cannot wait for Tyson to meet our little man. Mr. Tyson Bailey Jr," Delanie said smiling. Sadness spread over Kaydence's face as she remembered the message she was about to deliver to Delanie. "Have you gotten in touch with him Kay? When is he coming?" Delanie asked with much anticipation. Kaydence walked over and lay the baby in the hospital crib. "Well I actually spoke to—"

Storm

Kaydence struggled to place her mind in ready mode as she searched for the way to say what she was about to say to Delanie. Before she could continue her statement, the door slightly opened and a sudden cold front trickled through the room along with Mr. and Mrs. Bailey, Reverend Yasmin, and Charles. Mrs. Bailey went over to Delanie. As she was about to embrace her, Delanie felt a sense of coldness. The glare in Mrs. Bailey's eyes appeared lifeless. Delanie instantly knew that something was terribly wrong. "Oh

no please don't tell me something is wrong with

Tyson," Delanie said shaking her head in terror. Wells

of water immediately formed into the eyes of Mrs.

Bailey and were beginning to drip down her face.

Delanie could not sit to listen to the unspoken. She

jumped off the bed, tied her hospital gown and started

to head for the door. Reverend Yasmin caught her in

an embrace. "Honey there was nothing much the

doctors could do. They tried everything they could,"

Reverend Yasmin said tightly hugging Delanie. "Try

what? What did the doctors try? What are you saying?"

Delanie asked franticly peeling her body from the

embrace. She looked over at Mrs. Bailey and saw that

her face was buried into the arms of Mr. Bailey, it was

as if she was fighting back the cry. Mr. Bailey gently

rubbed his wife's back trying to comfort her. He too

wore the same lifeless eyes. Delanie was more

confused now than ever although she sensed

something was wrong, she was praying that it was not this wrong. "What is going on? Can someone please explain to me what is happening?" Delanie asked taking a step back, she needed to sit down. "I'm so sorry honey but Tyson is no longer with us," Reverend Yasmin blurted out before Delanie could sit. There was simply no right way to say it. Delanie sat and stared into a daze. She had heard Reverend Yasmin clearly and did not need any more clarification. "The doctors said it was congestive heart failure. It all happened too quickly and there was not much they could do to save him. Honey I'm so sorry but Tyson has gone on to be with the Lord. I can understand the—" Reverend Yasmin continued to speak because everyone else was in too much pain to say anything. Delanie listened attentively to every word Reverend Yasmin was saying appearing calm on the outside while fighting the storm of emotions forming inside of her.

Take It Off

Everyone was in her house. Aunt Helen was preparing food. Delanie had no recollection of how she made it from the hospital to her home. She had a vague memory of receiving her discharge papers. Now there were people in her house talking but their voices sounded like muffles. Delanie did not know how long she had been home. The scent of her baby was the only thing that could awaken her senses. Tyson's parents had taken care of the arrangement. His mother included Delanie in every detail. Delanie had been physically part of the process but emotionally she was disconnected. Her short black veil covered part of her face. Aunt Helen gently tapped her on the shoulders. "It's time honey. We have to go," Aunt Helen said as she helped her to stand. Delanie stood still she could not get her feet to move. "Baby girl I know it's hard but we have to go. Everyone is waiting on us," Aunt Helen whispered into her ears. The church was filled with blackness, everyone dressed in the color black. The casket was closed. The family members and close friends were seated in the front pew. Reverend Yasmin was already at the altar ready to begin as Delanie and aunt Helen joined the rest of the family in the front. "My dear beloved we are gathered here to celebrate the home going of our beloved son, father, husband, and friend—Tyson Bailey Sr. Tyson was an upright man not only a member of this church but—" Reverend Yasmin paused as she noticed Delanie walking towards the casket. Delanie approached the casket and tapped on it. "Open it," She demanded. The room grew silent. "Open it!" she screamed. Charles immediately got up and opened the casket he stood next to Delanie gently holding onto her arm. "Let me go," she said jerking her arm away from him. She stared at Tyson. He laid peacefully as if he was asleep. "Get up Tyson. Let's go," she demanded staring directly into his face. "Ty baby we need to go home.

Get up from in there." She turned to Charles. "He's not moving. Why isn't he moving?" Charles tried to hold her. "No! Tyson needs to wake up. Wake up you hear me!!!! You made a promise to me damn it! I just had your son, our son. He's here. Tyson wake up and hold our son. Stop laying in there! Who's going to help me with TJ huh? We're supposed to be raising our family. Tyson baby wake up. I need you to wake up. Get uuuuuupppppppp!!!!!" Delanie cried profusely screaming at the top of her lungs. Aunt Helen held her. "It's okay honey. It'll be alright," Aunt Helen said trying to console her. "No it's not okay! Nothing is okay! Nothing is ever going to be okay! I'm not okay!!!" She screamed and fell to the ground holding her chest. "This is not happening. He needs to wake up. I need him to wake up. Oh my God why is this happening? Why did he have to go?" She questioned. Death certainly took the life out of people, not just the deceased but everyone who is connected to them especially Delanie. She felt lifeless the moment her body hit the floor. She sat and cried her eyes out with one hand firmly gripped onto the casket. Everyone in the room had burst into tears. Delanie wanted to take off the pain. She needed to take off the sadness. This was without a doubt one of the saddest days of her life.

EPILOGUE

Blow

"You're here!" Delanie said running towards him. "I thought you left babe." She said tightly embracing him. "I've been here the whole time young lady just waiting on you," Tyson replied. Delanie blushed. "Dance with me," she said grabbing his hand. "Our song is playing," she started slow dancing to the music. Delanie was beaming with happiness. She rested her head on his chest tightly squeezing him as they danced. Her eyes began to flutter open. "Oh no," she sighed stretching on the bed. Over the years this had been their meeting place. Delanie wished she had an endless amount of dream dust she could use to blow on her face so she could fall asleep every time she longed to see Tyson.

"Happy birthday to you, happy birthday to you TJ," she sang as she walked into TJ's bed room with a cupcake and a candle with the number five lit over it.

TJ's smile widened. "Thank you mommy, can I eat it now?" "Of course you can baby but first make a wish and then blow out your candle," Delanie said as she sat on the bed with him. "Okay. I wish I had—" she interrupted him before he could continue. "Baby mommy can't hear your wish or else it won't come true remember?" Delanie reminded him. "It won't come true anyway mommy," TJ replied. "What do you mean baby?" Delanie asked with concern. "Because I wish I had a daddy." Delanie was stunned her heart dropped. TJ had never asked about a daddy before and honestly she did not mention anything to him about Tyson because she felt he was too young to understand. She also did not know how to tell him. They say five is the age children begin to remember things, so now was the time for TJ to hear about his amazing father. "You do have a daddy baby," Delanie told him. "I do?!" TJ asked excitingly. "Where is he?" TJ jumped off the bed anxiously. Delanie took his hand and took him into the attic. "He's in the attic mommy?" "No baby...well yes and no, pictures of him." "But where is he? I want to meet him," TJ asked again. "You do meet him every day," Delanie told him. "I do?" TJ asked perplex. "Yes baby, you do. Every time you look in the mirror you meet him. You are a trace of him. You carry him in your heart. We both do," Delanie kissed him on his cheeks. TJ smiled, he enjoyed receiving kisses from his mother. Delanie pulled the box marked "Tyson," placed TJ on her lap and began to show him things and pictures of his father. It's been a very long time since she looked at actual pictures of Tyson. She had even taken their wedding pictures and boxed them in the attic. Delanie only wanted to stay with the pictures of him she carried in her mind. She did not think she could bare to look at actual pictures of him but today was different. Today she looked at his pictures and talked to her son about the man he never met, the man who helped to create him.

The End!!!!

ABOUT THE AUTHOR

Geneva Kpangbai Diwan was born in West Africa, Liberia. She moved to the United States at the age of thirteen with family. She obtained a Bachelor of Arts in Communication Studies and Bachelor of Science in Human Development and Family Studies with an emphasis in Child Development from the University of Rhode Island.

Geneva enjoys reading and developed a love for story telling at a very young age. She currently resides in Rhode Island with her husband and works as a Head Start Teacher in Providence. In 2014, she began the journey of writing, "Time, Trial, Trust" and completed it in 2017. On her spare time she writes poetry and children's books, which she plans on publishing. Geneva loves writing and it is her desire to continue to share her stories with the world.

92013079R00157

Made in the USA
Columbia, SC
27 March 2018